"Gene O'Neill has been a fabulous writer for a long time now, and *A Stick of Doublemint* just adds to his rock-solid reputation. Highly recommended!"

—John R. Little, author of *The Murder of Jesus Christ* and *The Memory Tree*

"Nostalgic noir at its best! Author Gene O'Neil redefines hard-boiled with Private Investigator Katy Green in *A Stick of Doublemint*."

—Rena Mason, award-winning author of *The Evolutionist* and *East End Girls*

A STICK OF DOUBLEMINT

Book 4 in the series,
THE CRIME FILES OF KATY GREEN

by Gene O'Neill

<u>THE CAL WILD CHRONICLES</u>

The Burden of Indigo (2002)
The Confessions of St. Zach (2008)
The Near Future (2015)
The Far Future (2015)

<u>THE CRIME FILES OF KATY GREEN</u>

Book #1: Double Jack (2011)
Book #2: Shadow of the Dark Angel (2009)
Book #3: Deathflash (2010)
Book #4: A Stick of Doublemint (2020)

<u>OTHER NOVELS</u>

White Tribe (2007)
Lost Tribe (2008)
Not Fade Away (2011)

<u>COLLECTIONS</u>

Ghosts, Spirits, Computers & World Machines (2000)
Rockers, Shamans, Manakins & Thanathespians (2001)
The Grand Struggle (2004)
Collected Tales of the Baja Express (2006)
Taste of Tenderloin (2009)
In Dark Corners (2012)
Dance of the Blue Lady (2013)
The Hitchhiking Effect (2015)
Lethal Birds (2016)
Frozen Shadows & Other Chilling Stories (2017)

A STICK OF DOUBLEMINT

Book 4 in the series,
THE CRIME FILES OF KATY GREEN

by Gene O'Neill

with illustrations by Greg Chapman

and series afterword by Gord Rollo

and exclusive interview by B.E. Scully

DARK MOON BOOKS
Los Angeles, California

Interior layout by Eric J. Guignard
Cover design by Eric J. Guignard
www.ericjguignard.com

Front cover artwork by Jelena Mišljenović
www.instagram.com/jelena.misljenovic

Interior illustrations by Greg Chapman
https://darkartiste.wordpress.com

First edition published in June, 2020
Library of Congress Control Number: 2020931177

ISBN-13: 978-1-949491-23-4 (hardback)
ISBN-13: 978-1-949491-18-0 (trade paperback)
ISBN-13: 978-1-949491-19-7 (e-book)

DARK MOON BOOKS
Los Angeles, California
www.DarkMoonBooks.com

Made in the United States of America

(V041820)

This book is dedicated to:
Mu Chuisle

Chapters

*The essential American soul is hard, isolate, stoic,
and a killer. It has never melted...*

*The only justice is to follow the sincere intuition of the soul,
angry or gentle. Anger is just, pity is just, but judgement is
never just...*

—D. H. Lawrence

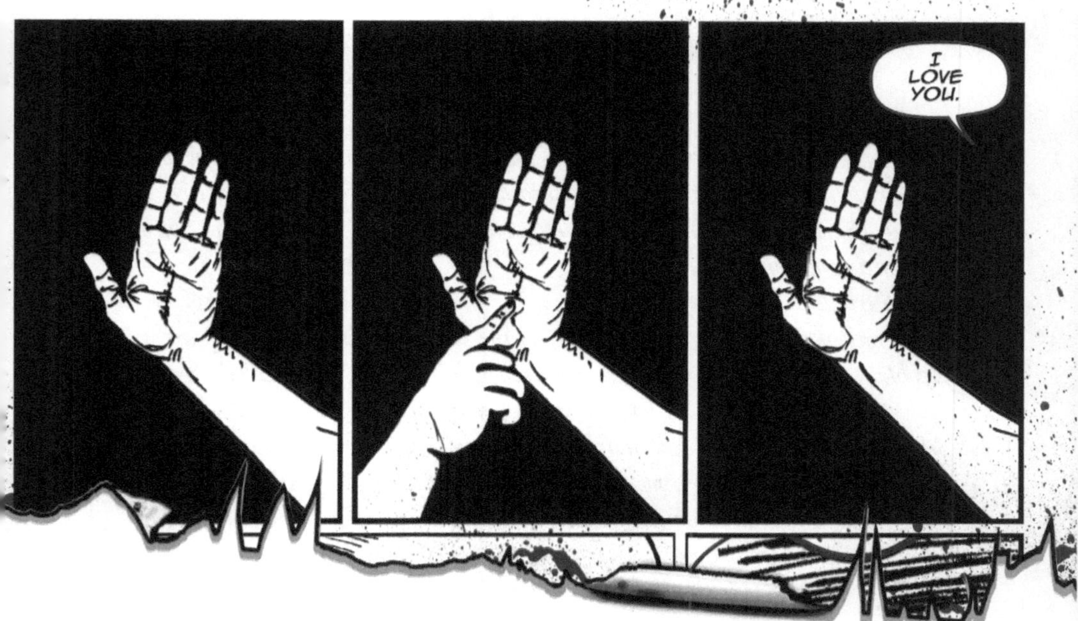

PROLOGUE

―――――――

MARINE CORPS RECRUIT DEPOT—SEPT 1ˢᵗ

*T*he senior drill instructor dismissed the entire platoon for ten minutes to write their first letter home. The sweating recruits dashed into the squad bays of the barracks, dug out writing gear from their foot lockers, sat, and started scribbling.

But you veered off into the head for privacy, sat in a stall, and communicated in a different way. You placed your forefinger into a slightly cupped palm and made a circling clockwise motion, as if dialing an old rotary phone. Your palm tingled, and soon you held it between your ear and mouth and said, "Hello, it's me."

"Oh, it's so good to hear your voice. Are you okay?"

"Yes, I'm fine."

"The routine not too harsh down there... not too hot or too physically demanding?"

"Not physically demanding. The obstacle course was tough for the first few days, but little more than an early morning jog now. It's fairly warm and humid here in the early afternoon, but scorching hot any time we have to spend out on the grinder during sunlight—"

"Grinder?"

You chuckled. "Sorry. The grinder is the nickname for an entire square mile of flat black asphalt used for lots of formal things, like parades, graduations, inspections, and such. But it's where all boot platoons spend daily hours and hours of close-order drill—what you civilians call marching. The grinder traps the heat, and is easily over one hundred and ten degrees when standing out on it during the day."

"Your whole situation sounds terrible."

After a bit of a pause: "Not too bad, really. Time passes fast here, as we're always kept busy, physically and mentally. Never a moment to ourselves, this ten minute break to write letters very unusual... Ha, at night I climb into my rack— that's a bed—planning to think about you and all our good times for a few minutes. But I'm out as soon as my head hits the pillow, not waking again until five-thirty when the D.I. startles everyone awake banging on a squad bay garbage can with a swagger stick. Anyhow, I now know I can survive anything they throw at us."

"Good, that's a relief. Been worried sick not hearing anything... I miss you so much. When will I see you again?"

"After boot camp, we have several weeks of ITR, Infantry Training Regiment. Every Marine goes through ITR before going on to a school or their first duty station. I've passed all the physical and mental tests and hope to be sent to Pensacola for flight training. But I'll get ten days leave at Christmastime before going to Florida or anywhere else after finishing ITR."

"Christmas seems a long ways away."

You said, "Not really... USF still good?"

"Great. You'd love my upper division American Literature class. We're studying Truman Capote's fiction techniques used in his non-fiction book, In Cold Blood. *We read something about that in English Honors, back in high school, remember?"*

"I do. Your American Lit class sounds like something I'd like."

"And I also love—"

You heard the D.I. shouting out in the nearest squad bay: "Platoon Twenty Thirty-seven, your writing time's up. Outside on the grinder. Right now!"

"Got to go," you said, jumping up. "Bye."

"Goodbye."

Abruptly you cut off the connection, dropped your hand to your side, and you hustled outside with the rest of the platoon.

ONE

At his best, man is the noblest of all animals; separated from law and justice he is the worst.

—Aristotle

An exceptionally warm day for early Fall. Normal evening mist blew in late from San Francisco Bay, doing little to chill the beginning of street activity in the Tenderloin. The humid ground air was still warm, tingling electric, itching, and full of tantalizing ethnic food smells drifting from open restaurant windows: exotic Afghan, spicy Mexican, and heavy Indian curry. Sidewalks crowded with many folks, most walking about in T-shirts, a few in shorts and tank tops; and a heavily-bundled scruffy old man, having an animated conversation with a parking meter, stood out in the skimpily-dressed crowd.

Streets were packed with traffic, everyone testing horns. Loud music blared from wide-open doors of bars—the distinctive growl of Joe Cocker wondering what you'd do if he sang out of tune. A siren roared like an angry lion on Van Ness. The time for heavy buying and selling neared, perhaps a half hour or so away—the regular nightshift of small-time hustlers, junkies, dealers, hookers, con men, and such, beginning to stir from their dens.

2.

Qwik Mart was located on the fringe of the Tenderloin, next to the narrow mouth of an alley half a block from the southwest corner of Geary Street and Hyde. Three dudes, dressed alike in tan pants and black T-shirts, loitered near the front entrance to the convenience store: a tall guy standing next to two smaller dudes sitting on milk carton crates, passing around a yellow plastic lemon bulb and a twisted paper bag containing a pint of white port. They drank, laughing, and signifying loudly on each other's families:

"Ya sista so ugly, she hasta sneak up onna drinka water," Little Richie said, the smaller of the two seated.

Repeat, the tall guy standing next to him, replied: "Y-Y-Yeah, and ya sista, s-s… " Pausing a moment, he stomped his foot to break the stammer, then continued, "She stoop foh the group, m-m-man."

"Ya brutha suck the big Juan."

"Ha. Y-y-ya mama so fat take five m-minutes to walk around her."

The husky one, Triple J, seated at the curb of the alley closest to the convenience store entrance, bent over and roared with laughter. He straightened, took an eye-watering hit of lemon juice, and chased it with the lip-smacking sweet taste from the bottle in the paper bag. He passed everything to Repeat, then put his hand up in the stop gesture as an attractive young woman appeared in the doorway.

Arlette James: blonde-flecked brown hair, tall, athletic, stylishly dressed.

She pressed a plastic grocery bag and a cocoa-colored tiny purse against her matching blouse. After enjoying dinner with her boyfriend at the *Afghan Kebob House* on Geary, she now watched Hyde Street traffic for his returning car; he'd dropped her off at the convenience store and was circling back around the block. With her free hand, she tried to slip something out of her purse as she struggled holding everything, all while keeping an eye on the traffic.

Triple J signaled her to stop, and finally caught her attention when he leaned close and waved his other hand.

"Whoa, whoa, whoa, pretty lady, whatcha hurry—"

At that moment, brakes squealed as an older green Honda—an obvious beat-up survivor of the San Francisco parking wars—peeled around the corner from Geary Street, slowing to a crawl. A young woman with tightly corn-rowed hair sat behind the wheel. Two men with red-checked bandanas covering their lower faces leaned out, each extending a 9mm Glock, cranking off multiple rounds rapid-fire.

Pop-pop-pop-pop-pop-pop-pop-pop.

The shooters quickly pulled themselves back inside. The nervous driver stomped the accelerator, the Honda fishtailing out of control. They swerved onto the sidewalk, narrowly avoiding a telephone pole but scraping a parked vehicle. A scattered crowd of pedestrians scrambled to safety, into the street or cramming into nearby storefronts. The driver miraculously gained control without hitting anything else, cut sharply back onto the street at the intersection of Hyde and O'Farrell, and sped off into the foggy night.

The two seated men, Little Richie and Triple J, and the woman, Arlette, had all been hit by gunshots, fallen and groaning and bleeding on the sidewalk.

Remarkably, Repeat still stood on the curb in front of Qwik Mart, untouched. A moment too late, he harmlessly threw the lemon bulb and bagged bottle at the rapidly departing Honda.

"Y-Y-You Wolfpack m-m-mothahfuckahs!"

Almost a month later, after a pair of operations, Triple J, who had survived being hit in the lower abdomen and upper thigh, recovered in the hospital; but Little Richie and Arlette James had both died that night of the shootings—Richie in the ambulance on the way to the hospital, and Arlette two and a half hours later in the intensive care unit. As soon as he was able to talk, Triple J insisted he didn't know the identity of the shooters.

3.

Standing as fire watch at your squad bay head, late at night with everyone else asleep, you felt an electric tingling in your hand. You placed a cupped palm between your ear and mouth and whispered: "Yes, I'm here. Is something wrong?"

For a few moments, nothing but the distant sound of faint static.

"Can you hear me?" you asked, not trying to hide your growing anxious concern.

Then, a barely audible whisper, far off: "Yes."

A woman's voice.

"Are you okay?" you blurted out too loudly.

"No, I'm not. They've shot me—"

"Who shot you? Where are you?"

No answer for what seemed an eternity. Then, an even fainter whisper: "Hospital, but I'm so tired and fading away into blackness… "

"Wait, wait—"

But the tingling in your palm suddenly blinked out.

From the fading last words and the sudden disconnect, you suspected she was gone.

Shocked, you covered your mouth, and with tears rolling down your cheeks, you whispered hoarsely, "I love you."

4.

An hour later, after the loud and lethal shootings in front of the convenience store and the arrival of the ambulance, the Tenderloin had settled back to normal, as if the descending thick mist were a shroud shielding the crowd from the results of the sudden violence. And the buying and selling cranked back up again big time on its streets and alleys.

5.

Also, an hour or so later, before relieved from your fire watch, you realized she was remarkably still alive, whispering from her hospital bed. "I'm weak, my vital signs are not too good… Daddy visited very briefly, angry, and he swore revenge. Too late for me to experience, I'm afraid. I'm fading into icy blackness again… Love you."

TWO

Nobody can give you freedom. Nobody can give you equality or justice or anything. If you are a man, you take it.

—Malcolm X

After almost a month had passed, not one suspect had been apprehended in the Qwik Mart shooting. Some critics claimed the San Francisco Police Department was dragging its feet because authorities had decided it was *only* black gangbangers killing other black gangbangers. Homicide had reinforced this view, determining the shooting was part of an ongoing pattern of recent rival gang violence between The Western Addition Wolfpack and 17th Street Black Knights. All the active Wolfpack and Black Knights, including Repeat, had guiltily disappeared from the street, going to ground below the police radar.

2.

Kenneth Jackson had transferred three years ago from the Narcotics Division of SFPD over to the larger Narcotics Division in the Oakland PD. Although he'd been living in the East Bay for the past ten years, and going back and forth over the Bay Bridge for the first seven, the work transfer to Oakland finally ended the daily commute. But Jackson knew he still retained a number of good friends on the police force in San Francisco. Perhaps more important, he hoped he still retained a few of his best CIs—Confidential Informants—from his once large network of street contacts in The City, who had been scattered about the Tenderloin, Mission, Western Addition, Haight, and Bayview-Hunter's Point.

After the *Chronicle* article announced no SFPD Homicide progress during the last four weeks, it took Jackson less than a day to validate that it had indeed been a Wolfpack gang shooting. The surviving victim, Triple J, and Repeat, who hadn't been hit at all, were known members of the Black Knights.

Jackson then only needed a little more than twenty-four hours to pinpoint detailed descriptions and street names for the two Wolfpack shooters: Baby Jr. and Black Diamond. Both gunmen had long juvenile rap sheets, and Black Diamond had been recently released on probation after serving twenty-three month's incarceration at Chederjan Youth Correctional Facility in Stockton for aggravated assault with a weapon.

Two days later, Jackson had dug up a supposedly secret Saturday night location, where Baby Jr., as a senior gang member, would be overseeing a new Wolfpack member's initiation party in a rented house off Potrero Street south of the Mission.

3.

Ken Jackson was a lean, athletic-appearing, middle-aged man, with gray-streaked brown hair. He was almost distinguished-looking, except for a faint hooked scar that ran from his cheek bone—below the corner of his left eye—and disappeared into the left corner of his mouth, giving him a rugged, tough look. Ironically, the scar was the result of a bicycle accident when he was only fourteen, long before any dangerous police work.

He sat patiently in his Ford Escort for over an hour, intently watching as the apparent last pair of party-goers disappeared into the shabby two-story residence at midblock. No streetlights nearby, but Jackson's eyes had adjusted to the darkness. Loud rap music blared out from the open windows of the house.

Jackson had lived near this once middle-class neighborhood ten years ago, before his nasty divorce and subsequent move over to Oakland. A few good early years when his kids were little. But his marriage had deteriorated after his strong-willed wife came to the decision that she was unwilling to deal any longer with the stress of being a cop's wife. It had come to a head when Jackson's long-time partner had been shot dead. The two were involved in what began as a routine drug bust outside a South of Market shooting gallery.

I can't stand knowing that when you go out the door, you may not be returning that night. I've been having terrible nightmares... You need to get another job for my sake, Kenny, something safer.

But Jackson never seriously considered quitting his job. He was dedicated to the Bay Area law enforcement's War on Drugs, in which he firmly believed.

And after an escalating series of fierce arguments, some stopping just short of turning physical, he and his wife had finally divorced, on very bad terms. She petitioned the court and, despite his attorney's best efforts, received full-time physical custody of both kids. She soon married a successful stock broker from Montgomery Street, and moved to the upscale Pacific Heights neighborhood. The youngsters eventually took on their mother's new last name.

The time slowly crept up on midnight, the party finally busting up after a visit by a pair of uniformed patrolmen. Neighbors had probably called in a rowdy noise complaint. Jackson slumped down in his car as a group of maybe a dozen people came streaming nosily down the steps from the two-story house, separated at the street, and piled into nearby parked cars.

Jackson perked up suddenly as Baby Jr. appeared, lagging way behind the departing group. The gangbanger paused on the top step, looking furtively about in the spooky darkness, before he nodded goodbye to the couple remaining at the door, the temporary tenants of the shabby house. He continued down the steps and hurriedly crossed the street to a Toyota parked directly across from Jackson's old Ford. Before Baby Jr. reached his ride, though, Jackson had quietly slipped out of the Escort into the cool, foggy night, drawing his .357 Magnum—an untraceable automatic he'd confiscated two years ago during an Oakland street drug bust.

He shouted, "Stop! Police. Hands up."

The gangbanger froze after spotting the weapon.

Jackson moved closer, asking for identification.

"Reach back with your right hand, take your wallet out of your pocket with your thumb and one finger… and do it very, very slowly."

Baby Jr. followed the lawman's instructions, his hand slowly reaching to his back pocket, putting him in a slightly awkward position, his dominant hand occupied behind him. But the gangbanger quickly twisted around to squarely face Jackson, fumbling for a Glock handgun. He withdrew the piece from an inside pocket of his coat, the microsecond delay costly—

Ping.

The characteristic, high-pitched, ear-splitting sound of a .357 automatic discharge.

Jackson had shot the gangbanger in the lower chest before he could level his weapon and get off a round. Then, Jackson quickly stepped in closer, bent over the groaning Baby Jr., and put another bullet into his forehead.

Sill leaning over the body, Jackson reached into the pocket of his coat, placed a wrapped stick of Doublemint gum into the dead man's open palm.

He picked up his two pieces of brass, then glanced up at the party house.

A moment or two later, after thinking he saw a shadowy movement in the small picture window, he retreated to his Ford and sped off.

Jackson did not experience a twinge of guilt over the killing of the gangbanger, which surprised him.

4.

Black Diamond was a bit more difficult to locate, staying out of public view, apparently worried as much about gang retaliation as a police arrest. He cautiously moved from friend-to-friend's apartments every few days, mostly in or near the Western Addition Projects, Mission, or Tenderloin, always a step ahead of Jackson.

But, nine days after killing Baby Jr., Jackson finally received solid information from one of his most reliable street contacts, Shaggy Pete, a small-time hustler and, on occasion, a four-for-one dealer—junkie sells four bags, then he gets a free one from the dealer.

From a conversation with Shaggy Pete, Jackson was able to pinpoint Black Diamond's current location: a girlfriend's apartment in the heart of the Projects. The girlfriend worked at a downtown Burger King during the eight-to-four early day shift.

On Tuesday afternoon, Jackson, wearing a brown UPS uniform, knocked on the girlfriend's apartment door. He held a small parcel in hand, smiling broadly.

Black Diamond peeked out of a side window, then a few seconds later opened the front door and said, "Yeah, man, whatcha—?"

Ping.

Jackson shot him in the head with his .357, then took a moment to place a stick of wrapped *Doublemint* gum in the dead gangbanger's hand.

He picked up his brass cartridge, casually strolled back to his old Escort, and departed.

Again, no feelings of guilt.

The responding pair of SFPD homicide detectives assumed the shooting was gang-related. They made no further effort in confirming their speculation, one way or another, or for making the important leap connecting the Qwik Mart shootings from several weeks ago.

5.

It took Jackson almost a week to track down the driver in the Qwik Mart shootings. Street eye-witness contacts had described a thin, attractive, well-dressed driver—a young woman with corn-rowed hair—but they could not help him come up with a name or address. And no young women with juvenile records fit the clean-cut description, nor did any female member of the Wolfpack or any other local gang. But there *was* a member of the Wolfpack who had a sister about the right age. Jackson pursued this lead further, and the gangbanger's sister indeed fit the witnesses' description of the driver. After digging a little bit deeper, he finally turned up her full name and a DMV photograph.

Irma Robinson—a good student, a sophomore and sprinter on the track team at San Francisco City College, hoping to attend SF State in the Spring of next year and run track.

Jackson wondered why she drove the car in the shooting, though. She had never been arrested as a gangbanger or involved with dope in any way he could determine.

He discovered the answer after more poking around. Irma's older brother was wheel-chair bound, partially paralyzed from the waist down after a Tenderloin shooting in a drug territory fight last Spring with the Black Knights.

This information made little difference in his plans. It only quelled his investigator curiosity.

At two-thirty in the afternoon, Jackson found himself in one of the City College's parking lots restricted for staff and students. He parked down several cars from a beat-up green Honda—the description fitting that of the car driven away from the Qwik Mart shooting. He settled in his Escort and waited patiently for Irma to finish her last afternoon class.

Finally, the neatly dressed, attractive young woman, with corn-rowed hair and wearing a Wonder Woman backpack, appeared in the parking lot. She stopped at the driver's door of her Honda, slipped off the backpack, and dug out her keys.

"I'm sorry, Irma," Jackson whispered, a hoarse catch in his voice, as he came up behind the young woman.

Irma jerked around at the sound of the strange male voice.

"Who are—?"

Ping.

He shot her in the heart with the .357.

Jackson picked up his spent cartridge, placed a stick of wrapped *Doublemint* in the young woman's hand.

He looked about, spotting several students entering the front end of the parking lot who may have seen what had happened. He wasn't sure. Jackson hurried back to his car, then sped away from the group of students, exiting the rear end of the parking lot.

A few minutes later, Jackson felt a momentary twinge of conscience well up. The clean-cut Irma was about the same age as his daughter, Arlette.

6.

There was only one responsible person left to find and eliminate: the Wolfpack's half-black, half Native-American leader, known on the street only by his preferred nickname, Breed.

The legendary shot-caller had no full name, no criminal record, no available photographs on file anywhere, and no known home address. Jackson's street contacts were at a complete loss to pinpoint the leader at any of the Wolfpack's preferred hangouts, or an identified apartment.

Breed was like a ghost fading into the foggy night.

Jackson began to wonder if Breed was a real person, or maybe some kind of gangland legend or myth.

THREE

I always believe, with any kind of hero, that you want to believe that their decision making is right. That ultimately, I can trust what that guy's sense of right and wrong will be. Even in a vigilante movie, where you are going against the law by definition, you still want to agree with the fact that your character is breaking the law.

—Lorenzo di Bonaventure

Katy Green was at her writing desk in the Marina apartment on Chestnut Street she shared with her longtime boyfriend, Johnny Cato.

She was a tall red-head, her appearance and graceful movements resembling those of a track high-jumper or volleyball player or other kind of athlete rather than the stereotyped nerdy, sedentary writer. And, indeed, while in college, majoring in Police Science, she had been a good basketball player for Sac State. Right out of college, she went to the police academy; and, then, after graduating, Katy was hired by Sacramento PD. She was assigned to a burglary unit for eight or so months and then to vice, where she was stuck for over four years. She'd finally achieved her preferred assignment goal in Homicide and had served as a detective her last five years.

But she was a successful professional writer now, starting first draft work on *Beyond Pandemic*, the second book in a two-book series she was calling The White Plague Chronicles. She'd finished the second draft of *The Sarawak Virus*. The first book took place in Borneo, Tasmania, and Israel. Places she and Johnny had visited in the last eight years since leaving their jobs with the Sacramento PD, where they'd been successful Homicide detectives.

The *Sacramento Bee* had dubbed the pair "The Green Hornet and Cato" after clearing eight major homicide cases, including running down the infamous "Double Jack."

They'd both experienced serious injuries during the apprehension of the notorious killer, and eventually left the Sacramento PD after Double Jack's trial. But Katy had written full-time since moving to The City, with one brief interruption six or seven years ago to assist Johnny and his private investigator agency catch the young man eventually dubbed "The Deathflash Killer."

She stared absently out her window, debating whether to include two separate novelette pieces in *Beyond Pandemic*. Both had been solicited for independent press science-fiction anthologies that were never published. They took place in the more or less correct time period, and background, and both would fit neatly into the framework of the new book.

She decided she would blend in both, which would save her significant writing time—a total of 25,000 words, and they were already edited.

Katy continued looking out the window in deep thought, knowing she was long overdue for another vacation. While on a project, writers spent too much time in their heads, even when they weren't physically writing. A writer friend had suggested long ago at a convention panel, that maybe all full-time writers should have a day job—preferably only part-time, just a day or two a week. Get outside their heads in a fresh setting, if only for a few hours weekly.

The idea had made perfect sense to her. But after finishing and turning in a four-book series called The Cal Wild Chronicles last winter, she'd ignored the sound advice, mostly because of a large advance based only on an outline, and she jumped right into working on The White Plague Chronicles—

"Hey, Katy," Johnny announced loudly, coming in the front door of the apartment, "Hap and an old friend are here with me. Okay to come in?"

"Bring them in, pal," Katy answered.

Johnny led the visitors through the apartment and paused at the door.

He was nine years older than Katy's forty-one years. He was also lanky, athletic-looking, but with a rugged boxer's face—broken nose not set quite right, scars over both eyebrows. He'd been a middle-weight Golden Gloves champion as a high school senior. Later, he was an All-American light heavy-weight champ while attending Sac State, when the college was better known for its boxing program than its Police Science. After college, Johnny had decided to use his Police Science degree and became a cop, declining offers from two Sacramento boxing promoters to turn pro. But, during his last few years at the Sacramento PD, after he'd teamed up with Katy, he had kept up an interest in his sport by volunteering and training the Folsom Prison inmate boxing team in his spare time.

Johnny was trailed by Hap Sullivan, a heavy-set retired Burglary and Homicide detective from SFPD, and Johnny's partner in their successful private detective agency—Sullivan, Cato, & Associates. Hap strongly resembled the actor John Goodman; and he always had a signature stogie jammed in his face, usually unlit. He looked pudgy and slow moving, but was a sharp-minded, top-notch investigator, and surprisingly agile when the situation demanded it.

Katy's eyes lit up when she saw the third man trailing the other two. It was Harlan Bundy, an old homicide detective colleague and friend from Sacramento. They hadn't seen him for years, but Katy and Johnny had recently heard Harlan was going through a messy divorce and considering either retiring or perhaps transferring from Sacramento PD to SFPD. He didn't look the worse for wear, perhaps a little grayer, slightly older. Katy hadn't known until this moment he was actually in San Francisco. She got up and gave Bundy a big hug.

"How are you Harlan," she asked, "and working here at SFPD in the City now?"

He nodded and smiled. "Yep, homicide, same as up in Sacramento."

"How's everything going?" Katy said.

"Pretty good, thanks, except the rent here is way too high for living on a cop's salary," he said, smiling thinly, shrugging. "And the division here is short-handed, as we always were up in Sacto, too." After a short pause, he added, "I know you're doing well, too, because I just finished the fourth book in your Cal Wild Chronicles series. Great stuff, Katy. I especially liked the second, the in-depth psychological analysis of the Indigo Man. Johnny says there may be some serious movie or TV interest in the entire Chronicles series?"

She nodded, and replied, "That's right, my agent has negotiated an option with a small, independent production company located in Toronto. I just signed this week. May never turn into a series or a movie, though. Most options don't pan out. But the year-long option is worth a few bucks one way or another. It's in the bank." She turned and faced Johnny. "What are you all doing over here during the day, pal—none of you guys working anymore or what?"

Johnny smiled, pulled and rubbed his damaged nose, a habit whenever he was nervous or thinking hard on something. Shaking his head, he said, "Actually, Harlan's visit is kind of related to something he's currently working on."

"Oh, really, and what are you working on?" she said, looking back at Harlan.

He took a deep breath and said, "Well, I've been assigned a new murder case, but it actually involves *five* other murders that Homicide has informally lumped all together under the label 'black-gang related'. Because of that decision, the detectives assigned the other five cases aren't really doing a full-court press, focusing almost all their attention on the rest of their heavy caseload. My assignment is one of the last three murders, but, like the rest in the division, I'm loaded with other higher priority cases."

Katy chuckled dryly and said, "They aren't practicing Harry Bosch's creed 'Everybody counts, or nobody counts?'"

She'd remembered Harlan was an avid reader and liked Michael Connelly's crime fiction series featuring the L.A. homicide detective,

Harry Bosch. Bosch pursued each and every one of his homicide cases as having equal importance, regardless of the victim's lack of social status. Prostitutes got the same amount of attention from him as movie stars.

Harlan smiled thinly and shrugged. "No, not by my Homicide lieutenant's design, they're devoting almost all their priority efforts to other cases right now. Kind of dismissive of the gangbanger shootings as not being of equal importance."

"Okay, I think I get it," Katy said, frowning and glancing from Harlan to Johnny, who she knew had a good reason other than just social for bringing their old colleague home during the workday—something about these gangbanger murders.

Johnny shrugged slightly, nodded back toward Harlan, giving nothing away.

"I'm the new man in the department," Harlan continued, "but I don't agree with the general opinion of Homicide that these recent three killings are *just* black-gang related. My opinion, as the lowest man on the staff totem pole, makes about as much impact as a fart in a windstorm. So, I'm kind of working my case on my own, you know." He frowned deeply and added, "It's slow going with the limitations on my spare time and low priority for services."

Katy nodded, and asked, "If those three aren't gangbanger-related shootings, what do you think they are? Something relating to something else... But what?"

"Well, I think the first three shootings at the Qwik Mart were indeed gang related. But I don't think the series of three murders during this last month or so after the Qwik Mart are gang retaliatory. Not at all."

"What are they then?" Katy said. "Who do you think could be responsible and why?"

"I think it might be a very clever vigilante, because the planning seems significantly more sophisticated, and the actual hits more professional than a typical gangbanger shooting. For example, he doesn't drive by and just spray his shots in the general direction of his targets. No, he stalks his prey carefully. All his shots are precise, lethal hits. And, before leaving the scene, he takes his time to police his brass cartridges after the hit."

Katy's interest perked up. "A sharp vigilante hunting down gangbangers? Something like those... ah, Charles Bronson movies?"

"Something like that."

"What's this vigilante's connection to the first three shootings? You must think these recent murders are directly related back to those Qwik Mart gangbanger hits?"

"I'm not sure yet, but, yes, I think these most recent murders are directly linked back to the Qwik Mart shootings. Actually, I was kinda hoping Johnny and you would take an interest. Be kind of my pro-bono consultants. I definitely need some expert help."

Harlan knew Katy had a particular interest in the abnormal psychology of murderers. She'd majored in Police Science in college, but had a strong minor in abnormal psychology. Her advisor, Dr. Wright, was a renowned abnormal psychology professor at Sac State and a consultant with both the CHP and Sacramento PD. And Katy was kind of renowned throughout the department for possessing an uncanny psychological knack—almost a psychic ability—of being able to project herself into the shoes of some of the most notorious sociopathic or psychotic suspects.

More often than not, her projections and analysis uncovered important keys leading to cases eventually being solved, like the "Double Jack" killings. She'd felt the killer, described by witnesses as grossly overweight, might be motivated to become a member of a local Sacramento health and fitness club, trying to quickly lose some weight. She'd been right, soon identifying his club, which eventually led to his takedown.

Katy glanced over at Johnny, who raised his eyebrows and smiled, the look indicating his interest. They had never had a vigilante suspect in their homicide cases in Sacramento. But, if Harlan was right, the possibility of a vigilante operating in San Francisco intrigued her. In addition, this would be a good time to get out of her writing head.

Harlan added, "Anyhow, I know you're busy writing, and it's paying well finally, and I can offer no compensation, but I was just hoping that maybe—"

"I need a break right about now," Katy interrupted, "so I'm interested in helping you to check out a possible vigilante perp. *But*, you are also partially right. I only want to devote a minimal investment of my writing time right now. We do the analyzing and consulting, you do the grunt work, surveillance, and whatever time-consuming legwork in the field is required."

Johnny was smiling broadly in agreement. He'd probably figured she would turn down Harlan outright, too busy concentrating on her recently contracted two-book series.

She turned back to Harlan and said, "We all have P.I. licenses, but we are still civilians. You'll probably have to get explicit departmental approval for us to be consultants and active in any way with you in the field."

Harlan looked a bit sheepish. "Actually, I already have my lieutenant's permission to bring you three onboard, and he also got higher-up approval. They think highly of the P.I. Agency. And, of course, the legendary work of the Green Hornet and Cato up in Sacramento helped swing the approval. The brass thinks it'll be good P.R. helping divert some of the current negative public criticism of Homicide's priorities. They'll make the big announcement of bringing you three onboard soon at an upcoming press meeting."

Katy chuckled at Harlan's boldness. He had always been an outside-the-box thinker when they worked with him in Sacramento.

"We can help with some of the field legwork, Harlan," Johnny volunteered with a hand gesture and questioning look, hopefully including both Hap and himself. Hap shifted his stogie in his mouth from side-to-side, and nodded his agreement.

In the first year or two in San Francisco, after just getting started with the P.I. agency, Sullivan, Cato & Associates had struggled to avoid bankruptcy and establish themselves. They had taken on the *Deathflash* case as pro bono work for a brother of a junkie victim. But after they tracked down the killer, with Katy's help, and garnered significant media attention and credit, the agency became extremely busy. Yet, recently, after an exceptional run of six or seven successful and profitable years, they had experienced a dip in obtaining new cases. So, Johnny and Hap had some slack time on their hands.

"How about this for an initial game plan, Harlan?" Johnny suggested, taking the lead. "First, Katy can review your available paperwork, copies of Incident Reports, autopsies, and whatever else you have. Even the entire murder books if you can smuggle them out."

Harlan smiled and nodded his willingness to please and get the help he needed. "Can't get those murder books out right now, though. Against department policy, as you remember it was up in Sacramento. And I don't want to violate any rules, at least not yet. But, I have some reproduced copies of some of the important parts of the books in a folder file in my car. The IRs, autopsies, and a list of witnesses interviewed, most of them from the Qwik Mart killings. Also, the Black Knight survivor's full hospital statements. Material on the most recent killings is pretty skimpy. I'll bring what I have in, and we can copy it for Katy."

"Excellent," Katy said, smiling.

"Are we going to keep meeting here at your apartment?" Harlan asked.

"No," Johnny said. "Hap and I have an office back in a cluster of businesses off Geary Street up near Japantown. It will be more convenient to set up a formal progress board up there. More room, too. And we have computers, printers, copiers, scanners, almost everything technical needed to work the case."

"Well, if it's okay with everyone," Katy suggested, "let's meet up there at seven tonight. I'll have finished looking over Harlan's files, and perhaps have input to contribute by then."

"Sounds good, kiddo," Johnny said. Hap and Harlan nodded their agreement. Johnny continued his lead. "Okay, other initial assignments. Hap, maybe you can nose around SFPD, homicide and especially the gang unit, see if you can dig up anything extra on the Qwik Mart shootings, the specific gang members that were involved, and maybe something not in the reports on the more recent murders, too. Then, if time allows, check around and see if any of your CIs are still available on the street. I know you've used a few of them in the past, even on our P.I. work. I'll help Harlan run down and re-interview witnesses on the street during the Qwik Mart hits. We'll go over all the Incident Reports for the last three killings. Oh, while at headquarters, Hap, can you check if any recent witnesses have turned up?" He flicked at his nose, looked around. "Any questions or suggestions?"

No one had anything.

"Okay, let's get to work, people," Johnny said.

2.

Katy spent the afternoon carefully reading over the paperwork Harlan had passed on to her. She believed that often the homicide murder book in a case held important clues not obvious to investigators at first. So, in her homicide work up at Sacramento, she'd always read and reread and reread the murder books. She didn't have access to them with SFPD Homicide, but she still had substantial paperwork to study.

In the past, she also liked to spend as much time as possible with the victims at the murder sites before their bodies were removed. Projecting herself back in time, trying to get mentally into the mind of the killer: What he might've been thinking or doing before, during, and after the time of the murder. The victims at these San Francisco killings were obviously not available now. So she went over the autopsy reports. Not much pertinent, except the Qwik Mart victims were all hit by 9mm slugs—two different weapons, two shooters. The three later victims were all killed with .357 rounds from one weapon—implying a single shooter. Nothing else stood out in the reports.

She read over the Incident Reports, all written up by the first responding uniformed officers, and later IRs added by assigned Homicide detectives. And then studied the notes taken while interviewing witnesses. Quite a few from people on the street at the Qwik Mart shootings, very few witnesses listed at the other more recent shootings—three different times and sites.

It would be interesting to see what Johnny and Harlan dug up on re-interviews. Johnny was especially good at questioning witnesses.

She read the statement of the surviving gangbanger. Triple J said he hadn't recognized the shooters. That was to be expected. But he also said he didn't know the young woman who had been killed either—she wasn't a gangbanger. He was in closest physical proximity to her, but no one had asked *anything* about her in the initial interviews. Especially, what she was doing just before they were hit.

Arlette James was considered by Homicide detectives to be just an innocent bystander, exiting the store at the wrong time. Therefore she was of no actual evidentiary interest, or worth following up in the investigation. Katy figured it was important to spend time validating that hasty supposition.

She also noticed there were *four* potential victims in front of the convenience store. One not hit at all, but identified by one of the detectives. No one had interviewed Repeat to-date, and there was no recorded address or phone number listed.

Katy took a shower, made herself an egg salad sandwich, mulling over what she'd read in Harlan's file, before driving over to Johnny and Hap's office. While eating, she'd jotted down several questions in her notebook for the meeting.

<u>3.</u>

A little after seven, everyone was present at the P.I. office off Geary Street near Japantown. Johnny started off listing topic areas on what he and Katy called their "Progress Board," a large blackboard mounted on the wall behind Johnny's desk. Johnny carefully listed five topic areas, writing the headings in all capital letters, with notes underneath:

<u>VICTIMS</u>	<u>SUSPECT(S)</u>	<u>QUESTIONS</u>	<u>ANSWERS</u>	<u>MISC. DATA</u>
[Qwik Mart]	Wolfpack Gang			
Triple J (survivor)				
Little Richie				
Arlette James				
[Separate hits]	Vigilante (?)	Vigilante (?)		
Baby Junior				
Black Diamond				
Irma Robinson				

Johnny asked for individual's reports: "Hap, what've got for us so far?"

"Not much. Didn't have enough time on the street earlier tonight. Although I saw several contacts who are still active out there. I'll follow up on those three and any others I might spot tomorrow evening. There are several witnesses to two of the three most recent hits. The temporary tenants who rented the party house near the hit on Baby Junior. And three college students in the parking lot just after the female driver was shot. They all believe they saw only *one* suspect, a male driving an older car, possibly a compact. No one could identify the make of the car, except one person said that she thought it wasn't a Volkswagen. That's about it. Didn't have time to do the interviews in any depth. We should probably follow up on those."

"Okay," Johnny said, turning and writing under the category of SUSPECTS: *One suspect spotted in two of the murders*, and also added *Vigilante* on the board under: QUESTIONS.

He faced the seated group. "Harlan and I got around to finding and re-interviewing about three-quarters of the listed Qwik Mart witnesses. Got better descriptions of the shooters and driver—they fit the suspects: Baby Jr., Black Diamond, and Irma Robinson. We also got two witnesses telling us that the girl, Arlette James, had actually paused in the entryway of the store and was reaching for something when she was hit before she could move from that spot. What caused her to stop and get shot? The witnesses could not answer that question or identify what she might have been reaching for."

He underlined confirmation of the three Qwik Mart victims, including the survivor, Triple J., and listed under QUESTIONS the contents of Arlette's purchase.

"We tried to interview the clerk at the Qwik Mart," he said. "But he was off today, works only part-time on the nightshift, seven-thirty to midnight from Friday through Sunday nights. He's a San Francisco State College student."

Johnny rubbed his nose and asked Katy if she had anything to add after her reading of Harlan's working files.

"Yes," Katy said, "a couple of things."

She mentioned that the second series of three murders used the same .357—implying *one* shooter, and that the two shooters at Qwik Mart had both used different 9mm Glocks.

"I have some questions," she added, "that I think indicate some required follow-up. First, there isn't much included in the IRs about Arlette James. Nothing about her purchases in the store, and what she was taking out of the bag, causing her to pause before she was hit. Maybe important. So, we need to talk to that first responding officer. And, after hearing Johnny's report, we also certainly need to interview that night clerk at Qwik Mart. What did he sell the girl? What did he see before and during the shootings? After all, the store door was wide open because of the heat of the night. Did he see what the girl was taking out of her bag?"

After pausing, she added, "I'd like to go out with Johnny and personally talk to this part-time clerk. Also interview those five remaining witnesses not re-interviewed today. And... " She checked her notes. "I'd also like to re-interview those witnesses of two of the three follow-up murders, maybe see what more they can add. Including any more weight to our theory of *one* vigilante suspect. That's all I have for now—"

"Wait," she said, glancing again at her notes. "I didn't find follow-up on the gangbanger standing in front of Qwik Mart. The one who was *not* hit. No address, nothing about him in the paperwork. The Homicide detective assigned the case called him Repeat, an odd nickname. We need to quiz both the first responding officer and the detective who identified him."

Johnny added Katy's questions to the board, stared at the new additions, and tugged at his nose. He finally turned around, and made the various assignments for tomorrow, including him and Katy working together.

"Hap," he said, "you check your street contacts, including those not spotted today. Interview them all thoroughly. Harlan can go along with you, meet all of your CIs—contacts that may also be important for him in the future. See if you can nose around the department again. Something new might have turned up. Especially potential witnesses to the last three hits. And check out the Homicide detective who knew Repeat. Katy and I will check out that Qwik Mart clerk, and re-interview witnesses not contacted today. We usually discuss stuff as we travel. Maybe we'll come up with more questions, perhaps even an answer or two after hearing what the clerk and witnesses have to say. I know Harlan likes doing the same, Hap."

Hap nodded.

Johnny glanced around, then asked, "Questions?" and since there were no questions, added, "Okay, let's meet here tomorrow night, at eight-thirty."

Everyone agreed on the later meeting time.

4.

By early the next afternoon, Katy and Johnny had run down the five additional witnesses to the Qwik Mart murders. They uncovered nothing of special interest, until talking to the last, an older Vietnamese widow living in the 'Loin with her married daughter. Hyu Nguyen had been walking directly across Hyde Street from the convenience store, and described what she'd seen.

"You saw her try and withdraw something from that shopping bag in her last few seconds before being shot?" Katy asked.

The older woman shook her head. "No, push bag and purse this way." She pressed one hand against her chest, then slid her other underneath. "Reach purse, behind bag."

"And what did you see her take out of her purse?" Katy asked.

"Not see, car in way, and loud shots scare."

Katy nodded, thought a moment, and then added, "Well thank you, Mrs. Nguyen, I have no more questions for you—"

The woman held up a forefinger, said, "Man come after police, ask you same question."

"Another police officer?" Katy said

Mrs. Nguyen shook her head and shrugged.

"Never show badge. Not say who he was. Just ask."

Johnny said, "And he asked specific questions, like us, about the victim?"

"Yes, what I see. I show bag, purse to chest."

Katy asked, "And you told him that the girl paused and was taking something out of her purse, *not* the bag, but you didn't see what?"

The elderly woman nodded. "Yes."

Johnny looked at Katy and lifted his eyebrows. "What did he look like?"

"Tall man. Like you. Older. Gray hair. Mark… here." She traced a line from cheek to mouth on her own face.

"A scar?" Johnny asked.

The elderly woman nodded.

"Very good," Katy said, smiling. "We may need to ask more questions later about this guy. Maybe get a sketch artist to talk to you. Will that be okay, Mrs. Nguyen?"

"Okay," the widow agreed.

Interesting, Katy thought.

None of the Tenderloin witnesses had asked for identification. No one had challenged their lack of official status.

Later in the car, Katy said, with a bit of excitement edging into her voice, "This guy could be our vigilante, pal."

"He was definitely interested in the girl, Arlette James," Johnny said. "So, you may be right. And, if so, she's the direct link to the three subsequent vigilante hits on the Wolfpack."

Katy nodded. "I think, without a doubt, this is our most significant development so far. Someone from Arlette's family, or perhaps a friend, could be this avenging vigilante. Her long-time boyfriend is another likely person of interest. He isn't mentioned in any of the reports, was never questioned, even though he dropped her off at Quik Mart. And no one from Arlette's family has been interviewed at all. One of the Homicide detectives personally advised the mother that her daughter was a shooting victim, and that was it. A short visit, no questions."

Johnny nodded, flicking at his nose. "You're right, we definitely need to follow up on this James family and the boyfriend. We'll ask Harlan to get a sketch artist out to Mrs. Nguyen as soon as possible."

"Yeah," Katy said thoughtfully, "and we'll interview Arlette's family first thing tomorrow. Track down the boyfriend, too, and have a talk with him."

They found out the boyfriend's name the next day. Chandler Blackmon. He was a student, like Arlette, at USF. But they decided to interview him later, after talking to Arlette's family.

They finished their day on the street, re-interviewing witnesses to the most recent three murders. The only solid confirmation: the suspect was indeed *one* man—but only a vague description. Maybe driving an older compact car… So, they hurried back to Qwik Mart to catch the clerk before their office meeting.

Eugene Wong was waiting on a customer.

They waited. And then, after asking a few questions confirming that Wong was indeed there for the shootings, Johnny asked, "What exactly did you sell that young woman victim?"

"Well," the clerk said, pausing as he thought. "She was in a big rush, I remember, acting like someone was picking her up any minute. She'd hurried in and grabbed a package of Tampax. She darted right back toward the street, but stopped suddenly in the doorway—"

"Just that *one* item in her bag," Katy said. "Nothing else, right?"

"Right," the clerk replied.

"She reached into her purse," Johnny said. "Did you see what it was?"

"No, afraid not. All I could see was her back as she stood in the entryway. Then I was ducking behind the counter, after those gun shots. I didn't see much of anything else before the cops got here."

"Okay," Katy said, "pretty good recall, considering all the chaos that night."

"Alright, Eugene, thanks for your help," Johnny said. "We may have some more questions for you later on, okay?"

The clerk nodded.

Out on the street, Katy said, "We need to run down the cop who wrote the initial IR. There was nothing in his report about the contents of Arlette's bag or purse. Or much of anything except her name. Let's see if he knows what she had on her. Ask him about the guy who was not hit, and if Repeat hung around and said anything at all about what he saw."

"Right," Johnny said, checking his watch. "It's getting late. We need to get over to the office, kiddo."

5.

They got to the office at eight-thirty, a few minutes before Hap and Harlan. Johnny opened the meeting with important results from his and Katy's day.

"One Qwik Mart witness described the victim, Arlette Jackson, pausing and taking something from her purchase bag just a second before the shooting began. But another witness, Hyu Nguyen, seemed more reliable, and said the girl was actually taking something from her *purse*, pressed against her chest, which was behind the bag. She didn't see what it was, though. Perhaps, more important for reinforcing our vigilante theory, she also described a mysterious man tracking her down *after* the cops questioned her. She was able to describe him, said he asked specific questions about the girl. Why was she paused in that doorway? What was she was taking from her purse before being shot? Arlette and this guy may be our link to the last three shootings. It sounds like he knew her. So, theoretically, he may be our vigilante… Harlan, can you get a sketch artist out to Hyu Nguyen in the morning?"

"I'll set that up."

"Katy, you want to talk about the clerk?"

She described the interview with Eugene Wong as Johnny wrote things on the progress board. She mentioned that the girl had bought only one item, Tampax, and it was in the plastic bag. She'd stopped in the doorway for several seconds, which Wong confirmed.

Johnny turned and said, "There were only witnesses to two of the last three murders, and they were marginally helpful. The house renters little at all, except for saying they saw only one shooter. The three college students validated that only one shooter hit the girl, Irma Robinson. They weren't able to give a good description of his car, only that it was old and a compact. Anything else, Katy?"

"Yes, there's nothing much in the IRs or follow-up on Arlette, her family, or her boyfriend. We want to interview them. And someone needs to run down the guy who was *not* hit, the one the homicide detective called Repeat. Maybe that detective got an address, or knows how to contact him. *If* we can get him to talk."

Johnny made the necessary additions to the blackboard. He turned and said, "What do you guys have?"

Hap took his stogie out of his mouth. "Not much at headquarters, except another witness to the aftermath of the shooting of the girl in the parking lot. A City College history professor, getting in his own car after his three o'clock class. He thinks he saw the shooter's car pull away from him in the parking lot. Thought it might be an older Ford Escort, maybe tan or gray, but he didn't get the license plate." Hap checked his notes. "Nothing much from my street contacts. Although I spotted another of my CIs on the street, a part-time drug dealer and hustler named Shaggy Pete. Didn't get a chance to talk to him, but he's always reliable and sharp—one of my best informants. And an unusual bonus, he seems to always avoid incarceration, and so he's always available to talk. I'll run him down tomorrow, if possible."

Johnny nodded and wrote the suggestion and name under the MISC. DATA heading.

He turned and said, "Okay, assignments for tomorrow. Katy and I will interview the James family. May lead to other relatives or friends being contacted, including the boyfriend, Chandler Blackmon. Harlan, you get that sketch artist to accompany us in the morning to visit Mrs. Nguyen. You and Hap see if you can get an address for Repeat. Hap, also try to run down Shaggy Pete and any other street contacts you may spot. Someone out there has got to *know* something of significance. Find them."

He glanced back at the board, then said, "Does anyone have anything else they think needs checking out tomorrow?"

"Yes," Katy said, "we should check *all* the first responders again, uniform officers and homicide detectives, see what they remember but did *not* include in their IRs or follow-up reports. Johnny knows the officer responding at Qwik Mart. We'll see what he remembers, see if he talked to Repeat. Also, anything he didn't write in his IR on Arlette James."

It was obvious to everyone that Katy was caught up now in the heat of the investigation and was all in.

"Hap, if you have time, you two cover the rest of those other first responders," Johnny said. "That's it for tonight. Let's aim for seven again tomorrow night?"

Hap, Harlan, and Katy all nodded.

6.

Around two the next afternoon, Katy and Johnny had caught up to and interviewed Liam Rourke, the young police officer who wrote the first responder IR at the Qwik Mart shootings. Johnny had crossed paths with him during several previous P.I. cases, even had lunch once, so they were on pretty friendly terms. He accepted their informal status on the investigation with no comment.

Johnny said, "Liam, we see nothing in your IR on the victim, Arlette James."

The husky redhead thought a moment and replied, "Figured she was just an innocent bystander, Johnny, hit by stray bullets. The three black gangbangers were obviously the intended targets of the two shooters, you know. I didn't think anything could be important enough about the bystander victim, other than she was in the wrong place at the wrong time."

"That may be true," Katy said, "but you didn't even mention her bag and purchase, or her purse. Did you, by any chance, notice what was in them?"

Rourke scratched his head. "Well, of course I followed proper department procedure for first responders. I taped off the area, not allowing anyone to contaminate the murder scene, and waited for the homicide detectives, forensic techs, and medical examiner to get there. But, yeah, I noticed the plastic bag had emptied out on the sidewalk. A small package of Tampax. That's all there was in the bag. Only glanced at her purse: a wallet, lipstick… ah, maybe a cell phone and other small stuff crammed deeper inside, a roll of mints or something… but that's all I remember. If you think it might be important, I'll give it more thought, see if I can come up with anything specific. But that purse will be in a box at headquarters, in the evidence lockers labeled "Qwik Mart Homicides," if you do need to inventory its contents."

"Yes," Katy said, "if you remember, it might be helpful, could save us a trip."

They chatted a few more moments, getting nothing much of additional importance. Liam couldn't remember if the guy who was not hit had said anything. He noticed the Homicide detective assigned the case, though, knew the guy and had talked briefly to him.

Johnny said, "Thanks, Liam, appreciate your help. Call me if you recall anything else you saw, especially the purse contents."

7.

Margaret James was middle-aged, with her forehead heavily wrinkled and crows-feet at the corners of her eyes. Katy thought she'd been a very attractive woman in her younger days and would still turn heads. The woman answered the front door with an attractive smile and invited them into her home—a well-kept Victorian in upscale Pacific Heights.

Katy and Johnny identified themselves.

"Consultants on the Qwik Mart shootings, but not actually police officers," Mrs. James said, frowning a bit suspiciously. "That's kind of unusual, no?"

"It is," Johnny said, "but I can explain. But first let us express our sincere condolences for the loss of your daughter. Such a shame, with someone so young and with so much potential. We are very sorry."

"Thank you, we miss her terribly," Mrs. James said, dry-eyed, and with only the barest audible hitch in her voice. She was obviously a private person and stoic publically.

"We were homicide detectives up in Sacramento until a few years ago," Johnny explained, "and worked closely with one of your homicide detectives here on the case. We are now private investigators, but helping our friend in SF homicide assigned this case as pro bono expert consultants."

The woman tentatively nodded her acceptance of the explanation, but still retained some degree of concern that showed in her slightly frowning expression.

"We'd like to ask you a few routine questions, Mrs. James," Katy said. "Some about Arlette. A few about that terrible night. A little about your family. We'd appreciate your cooperation."

Mrs. James thought a moment, then replied, "Okay, fine."

"Your daughter lived here at home, right? Will you tell us a little bit about her?"

"Yes, Arlette lived here with me and my husband. She was in her junior year in pre-med at USF, wanted to be a pediatrician. Doing very well. An excellent student, and a pretty fair volleyball player on the varsity team, a starter. And... " She paused a moment to blow her nose, then added, "Sorry."

Katy waited respectively before speaking again, then asked, "And did Arlette have any other siblings living here at home with you?"

"No, she does have a sister, Annette, but she doesn't live here anymore," Mrs. James said, her tone noticeably stiffening. "She's estranged from the family, and we haven't seen or heard from her in over three years. We don't stay in contact with her at all."

Katy nodded, moving away from an obviously touchy family subject, focusing back on Arlette. "That night at the Qwik Mart, Arlette was on a date with Chandler Blackmon?"

"Yes."

"Was Chandler her regular boyfriend?"

"Yes, since they were seniors in high school. He was attending USF, too, a mathematics major, also a good student."

"He picked her up here for a dinner date," Katy said, "and was going to bring her back home afterward. Is that accurate?"

The woman nodded. "Yes, they both were studying for upcoming tests."

"And you, Mrs. James, you and your husband were at home all evening?"

"I was, but Tony had a late overseas conference call at his office on Montgomery Street. The firm is very busy at the moment, getting close to releasing an important new stock IPO."

"I see," Katy said. "About what time did Mr. James get home that night?"

There was a long pause, then Mrs. James said in a testy voice, "I don't understand these specific questions about me and my husband's whereabouts the night our daughter was murdered. Is it possibly of any relevance to anything in the investigation?"

"Let me explain, Mrs. James," Johnny said, smiling apologetically. "There have been recent murders of the three Qwik Mart suspects involved in your daughter's death. We don't think those recent shootings were by rival gang members, or retaliatory murders. We think that *maybe* a vigilante is seeking revenge for the shooting of your daughter. With that in mind, we are obligated to pursue this line of thought and ask of your whereabouts at the times of those three shootings. Do you recall where you and Mr. James were on Friday, at midnight, on the second of November; and Tuesday, November thirteenth at two in the afternoon; and, finally, on Tuesday, November twentieth at about two-thirty in the afternoon?"

Mrs. James face tightened into a deeper frown, and she said in a brittle voice, "Of course, *not*. I don't remember offhand without checking my personal calendar where I was on those dates and times.

But I must say that I resent this line of questioning. You're implying my husband and I are being considered as suspects after Arlette was shot and killed by these hoodlums. That's absolutely ridiculous. You have to be joking, right?"

"No, not suspects at all, just *persons of interest*, who are routinely questioned in any type of murder investigation." Johnny explained, shrugging with a smile. "Sorry if the questions seem invasive or suggestive of suspicion of anything. They're nothing more than routine in an investigation like this. You are part of a fairly wide range of people considered persons of interest. Any chance of you checking your calendar for those specific dates for us?"

Mrs. James didn't respond for a few moments, then said, "No, I don't think I want to go to the trouble to check my calendar for you."

There was a long, awkward silence.

Katy said, "Your husband must be at work today?"

Mrs. James nodded. She said in a sharp voice, "I suppose you are going to want to bother him at his office today?"

"Yes," Johnny answered.

"Well, I'm going to call and warn him of your forthcoming visit, and your lack of official law enforcement credentials."

"That's your right, of course," Johnny said to the obviously upset woman.

She moved by them toward the front door.

"Sorry for the aggravation, Mrs. James," Katy said. "We know it's a very difficult time for you."

The woman opened the front door, gesturing for them to leave.

Outside, Johnny said, "Did you feel that might've been a slight bit of an over-reaction, kiddo?"

"Well, it's only been a little over a month since she lost her daughter. Naturally, she's still upset. But she did seem to heat up even more after we mentioned her husband and those specific dates of the recent hits. Be interesting to see how Mr. James reacts to all this."

8.

They found the husband's address, a notable high-rise on Montgomery Street in the heart of what was considered the "Wall Street District of the West." Mr. James's office was on the top floor. The door was marked: *Burney, Harmon, James, and Associates, Investment Consultants.*

A striking auburn-haired young woman, dressed in a burnt orange suit and a pearl necklace, sat at a beautiful polished teak desk in a swanky, thickly carpeted, plush waiting room, which guarded the inner sanctum of offices down a similar thickly carpeted corridor behind her. Outside the array of expansive windows in the waiting room was a panoramic view of the Bay Bridge, spanning the water from San Francisco to Treasure Island, and from there continuing over to Oakland and the East Bay.

Johnny and Katy introduced themselves, explaining that they were here to see Mr. Anthony James on a routine police matter.

The young woman smiled broadly and said that Mr. Lippenstein, one of the firm lawyers, was expecting them, and would be right out. She hit a button on her phone bank.

Mr. Lippenstein came out to greet them with a thin, stiff smile. He wore an expensive dark blue English worsted suit and light blue silk tie.

"Hello, may I see your credentials, please?"

Johnny handed him his California State Private Investigator's License.

Mr. Lippenstein looked up with his fake smile, and handed back the license. He spoke in an obvious cold and dismissive voice. "Since Mr. James understands this is about his daughter's murder, he prefers to answer any questions from only *official* authorities assigned to the case, with, of course, the proper credentials. And I will be present at any future interviews. I'm afraid you two won't be able to speak to Mr. James today, or really anytime. Sorry for your waste of time… Maureen will escort you back to the elevator bank."

He waited for the receptionist to stand and come around her desk, then he disappeared back down the corridor of private offices.

"This way, please," Maureen said, leading them out of the waiting room.

Looking back at the building, Katy said, "Wow, we've been thrown out of some dives in the past, but never quite so rudely and quickly from such a swanky place as this, and by such a snotty-ass and dismissive attorney. We're slipping, pal."

"Yeah," Johnny said, chuckling, "and that lawyer looked like he goes strictly by the book, would never consider anything like even drinking milk directly from the carton, even late at night with no witnesses. It's interesting that Mr. James called in a lawyer *before* even talking to us or any detectives. Dude couldn't even extend the courtesy of seeing us himself?"

"Yeah, he deserves at least a double line under his name in our notes, and on the progress board," Katy said.

9.

Later that afternoon, they caught up with Chandler Blackmon at a three-bedroom apartment on Anza Street near the USF campus, which he shared with two roommates.

Chandler Blackmon was a pleasant young man, with no relevant information to help in their investigation. He saw nothing of the shooting, still stuck in traffic back on Geary Street. He thought maybe Arlette could have been taking her cell phone from her purse, but he'd received no message from her in those last few seconds before being shot. He was vaguely aware of the three recent gangbanger murders, but had no idea they were related to the Qwik Mart shooting.

Before they left his apartment, Katy noticed that the young man did not have a faded scar on the left side of his face. In fact, he had no scars, blemishes, or even a shaving nick on his face.

Nice-looking young guy, she thought.

"I don't think he's a good candidate for our vigilante," Johnny said.

"I agree."

10.

That night at the office, only Harlan showed up on time to meet Katy and Johnny.

"We ran Shaggy Pete down on the street just before time to get back over here," Harlan explained. "After a few words, Hap decided what he was hearing was going to be worthwhile enough to stay behind and do a thorough interview with his street contact. However long it would take. So, I took the car back. He'll be along soon, I think, catching a cab when he finishes talking to Shaggy Pete."

"Okay," Johnny said. "While we wait, why don't you bring us up to date on what you guys discovered today."

"We have an artist committed to go with you to see Mrs. Nguyen early tomorrow morning, first thing. You should have a finished sketch before lunch." He paused, checked his notes, then continued. "We interviewed all first responders, both uniform cops and homicide detectives. No address or phone number for Repeat. But, the detective assigned the murder of the girl driver, Irma Robinson, casually mentioned something intriguing. The victim had a wrapped stick of Doublemint gum clutched in her hand. One was also in *my* victim's hand. So, we checked with the other homicide detective, and he, too, had spotted the same thing—a stick of wrapped Doublemint gum. More than coincidence. The shooter may have placed the sticks of gum. But, remarkably, neither of the other two detectives thought it important enough to include in their murder book reports. *I* did. Thankfully, this fact hasn't been leaked to the press yet, or anywhere else. So, to date, we are the only ones in addition to those two other homicide detectives who are privy to this strange bit of information."

"Wow, that's interesting," Katy said. "Seems the shooter must've placed those sticks of gum for a reason. Any idea what it could mean?"

Harlan shook his head. "Not a clue. I'm open to any suggestions, though." He stared at them for a few seconds; then, when no one came up with any possible explanation, he cleared his throat. "Nothing else relevant remembered by anyone."

Johnny listed and underlined "Doublemint" under the QUESTIONS column.

Katy summarized their interview of Liam Rourke, then mentioned that Arlette's purse wasn't inventoried by Liam. She asked Harlan, "Your first responding detectives at Qwik Mart didn't inventory it either?"

Harlan shook his head and shrugged.

Johnny summarized their uncomfortable interview with Mrs. James and their interaction with his lawyer. And Katy was almost through explaining *why* Johnny was double-underlining his name under SUSPECTS when Hap came charging into the office.

The rotund investigator took the stogie out of his mouth and wiped sweat from his forehead. "Got some good stuff for you all," he said breathlessly. He'd apparently run back to the office after dropped off by a taxi out on Geary Street. After recovering, Hap continued. "I spent some productive time with my street contact, Shaggy Pete. He revealed some valuable information that he'd been run down and questioned some time ago by a guy looking for information on locating Black Diamond—"

"Did he describe the guy?" Johnny interrupted, excitement edging into his voice.

"Better than that! He identified the guy. Unfortunately, not with a name. But he had talked to him two or three times in the past. And get this! Shaggy Pete thought this guy had been an *undercover cop* back in the day in the SFPD narcotics section. He was a cop until a few years ago. Shaggy Pete said he hadn't seen the dude for probably three years, maybe longer. Then, suddenly, the guy pops back up, asking specific questions about identifying and locating the two Qwik Mart shooters and the driver. And then, after the recent murders of these three suspects, the guy appeared again, just the other night, asking specific questions about locating the Wolfpack's shot-caller, a legendary guy known on the street only as Breed."

"Shaggy Pete described this guy?" Katy said, picking up on the electric excitement.

"Yep, fits your Vietnamese witness's description to a tee, including the faint scar on the left cheek. No question it's the same guy, Katy."

"Okay, let's cool it a moment," Johnny said, while rapidly adding stuff to the progress board. "Katy and I will have a sketch of him from Mrs. Nguyen early tomorrow morning. Hap, let's get this Shaggy Pete into headquarters as early as possible, and get a sketch from him, too.

Then, you and Harlan can distribute reproductions of the two sketches to the narcotics section. We realize undercover guys in dope don't last on the street very long, but there may be a detective or two who might still be over there and can identify our guy. You can always take the sketches around to other departments and check with detectives who've been at headquarters for over three years. It's possible that some uniform cops may be able to recall him, too."

Katy felt the tingling in her stomach she'd always experienced when closing in on a suspect. Who was this guy? They weren't sure, yet. But, all thoughts about Anthony James as the potential prime suspect were on hold.

Everyone in the room was grinning with anticipation.

"Okay," Johnny said, after getting everything written onto the progress board. "We get our sketches of this guy done in the morning, meet here as early as possible tomorrow. I'm feeling really good about this Shaggy Pete's revelation."

||.

An hour and a half before lunchtime, Hap brought Shaggy Pete in to sit with an artist. Half an hour later, Katy and Johnny arrived, delivered the Nguyen sketch to Hap and Harlan. The drawings roughly matched, including the left cheek scar. They prepared numerous copies of the sketches of the suspected vigilante—a cop or maybe ex-cop—to spread around SFPD.

"You guys check out narcotics first, then maybe around the whole department. See if anyone recognizes this guy and can name him. Katy and I will meet you here as soon as possible. She has an important writing errand that has to be attended to today."

Around twelve-thirty, Johnny and Katy were back in the office eating roast beef sandwiches from nearby Fat Albert's, and waiting patiently for Harlan and Hap. As time crept by, Katy took her mind off the anticipated results of the sketches by studying the progress board. After carefully reading over the various sections, she had a nagging feeling in her gut that something important was up there, but unable to pinpoint exactly *what*…

Then she remembered that they still needed a location for the Wolfpack shot-caller, Breed, and to bring him in for questioning. If they didn't get much, as she suspected, she could at least warn him of the vigilante who may be stalking him.

But there was still something else important lost on the blackboard that would require follow-up. Something obviously non-descript. But, despite really concentrating, Katy couldn't spot it. She finally gave up and pushed it again to the back of her mind, knowing sooner or later it would surface from a vague nagging to a full-blown identifiable itch.

Later that afternoon, Hap and Harlan returned to the office, neither looking enthusiastic.

Hap said, "We only talked to a few guys in narcotics. Most of their cohorts were not even scheduled in until the early evening. The few available, mostly newer guys, could not identify our suspect."

Harlan added that they'd checked around with the department. No luck, so far. But headquarters had all its on-duty uniforms on the street, and almost all their investigators were out in the field by the time they began asking around. They'd go back over before five o'clock, try to catch some as they returned to punch out from their day shifts.

"Oh," Hap said, lifting his eyebrows and pointing at Johnny and Katy. "A possible good lead for you. There is a detective lieutenant, recently retired, who was a long-time supervisor in the narcotics division. The few guys in the office thought that if *anyone* would remember this guy, it would probably be Gus Pappadopulus. I knew him pretty well, personally. Good man. So, I took the liberty of calling him up, and he's expecting a visit from you two after six this evening. He's got a temporary gig working a day shift as a security supervisor at the Vallejo Fairgrounds during the racetrack betting season. Here's his Vallejo address. Harlan and I will go back to headquarters this evening, paper all divisions with copies of the sketches, and directly hit everyone we can punching out, and those punching in. See if anyone can identify this cop from either of the two sketches."

"Sounds good," Johnny said, taking the scribbled address.

Before they took off for Vallejo, Harlan called Johnny back. "No luck so far, but many of the robbery, burglary, and homicide detectives here start work later, almost as late as the narcotics guys, so they aren't back yet. No luck with the uniforms coming back off the day shifts, either. Haven't talked yet to most of the midnight shift. You guys check back in after you talk to Pappadopulus, okay? I'll keep you up-to-date if we get lucky and score a hit. Somebody's got to remember this guy, if he really was a cop in the recent past."

12.

Gus Pappadopulus was a divorcee, retired two years, and lived by himself in a rented studio apartment on East Georgia Street in Vallejo. He was better than being in just *fair* physical shape. A big man, well-muscled, his thinning dark hair only gray on the sides. He looked more like an aging football linebacker slowly fighting off middle-age than a retired sedentary cop.

He invited them in, pulled out high stools at a counter separating the tiny kitchen and dining area, and offered them a beer or soft drink.

Johnny joined him for a Sierra Pale. Katy took a can of Pepsi.

"Okay, down to business," Gus said. "I understand you're chasing down a murder suspect, possibly a cop, who you think may have been assigned to my department in the past, and you have some sketches of him. Right?"

Johnny said, "Yes, that's correct."

"Okay, let's see 'em."

Johnny handed over copies of the two drawings.

Gus grinned widely, lifted his eyebrows, and nodded. He handed back the sketches, holding one a moment longer.

"This one is best," he said, "but the scar pinpoints my guy in both sketches. His name is Kenneth Jackson. Worked for me in narcotics for maybe eleven or twelve years. He made Detective before he transferred to Oakland PD, and that was three or four years ago. I'm guessing he's still in narcotics. Anyhow, he actually moved to Oakland after a contentious divorce. Yeah, that must've been a little over ten years ago, as I recall. Never saw much of him after that move, even though he worked here at SFPD for about seven years after the divorce.

They chatted for a few minutes, until Katy realized from Gus's remarks that Jackson had once been married to none other than Margaret James. She asked in an excited tone, "He had a daughter named Arlette, right?"

Pappadopulus nodded, and indicated by pointing at his empty beer bottle, silently asking if Johnny wanted another?

Johnny shook his head.

"Actually, there were two kids, twins," Gus continued, "the wife getting full custody of both after the divorce. That court decision really upset Kenny. Probably a prime reason for his moving over to Oakland and commuting back here only for work."

Johnny said, "Tell us about Jackson, you know, personal stuff."

"Well, he was a good guy. Quiet, always got along well with the rest of the team. At first, he worked undercover for several years, that scar and long hair helping him look sketchy. He was really good at undercover, lots of arrests. But never any excessive rough stuff while he was on the street. Even received two department citations. After making Detective, he had to shoot a suspect, though, who'd attacked his partner with a knife. Kenny took that pretty hard. Internal Affairs quickly cleared him of wrongdoing." Pappadopulus rubbed his chin, thinking. "He was a firm believer in the war on drugs. Dedicated. Favored long sentences for dealers. All this is why I think he's probably still working in the narcotics division over in Oakland."

After a short pause, Johnny said, "That's all good background on Jackson, Gus, appreciate it."

"Do you feel he's capable of taking justice into his own hands?" Katy said. "Executing two gangbangers and the driver responsible for his daughter's death. Revenge killings?"

The retired cop thought long and hard. Finally, he frowned and nodded reluctantly. "Yeah, I guess he could do that. Especially if he believed there was a good chance those responsible might never be brought to justice. If he thought homicide was too busy, pushing these murders of black gangbangers and his daughter onto the back burner. Yeah, I think Kenny might be psychologically able to square up himself to the hits. Eye for an eye philosophy."

"That's more than just intriguing background," Johnny said. "Do you have an address for Jackson in Oakland?"

He shook his head. "HR at headquarters must have something, though."

Katy and Johnny slipped off the stools. They shook hands, thanking him for his help.

"If you remember anything else important about Jackson, call me," Johnny said, handing Pappadopulus one of his P.I. cards.

"Will do. Good luck."

On the way back to San Francisco from Vallejo, Harlan called and said, "Hey, we got lucky. We have a uniform and a pair of detectives that have all positively identified our guy—"

"I bet his name is Kenneth Jackson," Johnny interrupted, chuckling.

"The guy in Vallejo identified him, too?"

"Right," Johnny said. "See you both at the office soon,"

"Hap may be late again," Harlan said. "Shaggy Pete called and wanted to meet up. I think Hap slips him a few bucks for any good info after visits. Anyhow, he remembered the name of an old shot-caller for the Wolfpack, one who did a long stretch in San Quentin and just rose up again. Out on parole, permanently retired from the gang. This guy may be able to give Hap the legal name and other information on this Breed dude, maybe a location."

"That's good news, Harlan, see you soon."

FOUR

He saw very clearly how all his life led only to this moment and all after led to nowhere at all. He felt something cold and soulless enter him like another being. And he imagined that it smiled malignly, and he had no reason to believe that it would ever leave.

—Cormac McCarthy

Kenneth Jackson was at his duplex apartment in Oakland and digging into a vegetarian pizza when his cell phone interrupted his dinner.

"You recognize my voice, Kenny?"

"Yes."

"I owe you this heads-up for saving my ass in the old days. A retired SF cop you don't know, and a new homicide detective who just transferred from Sacramento PD, are circulating around headquarters two police artist sketches of the hitter of the three Qwik Mart gangbanger suspects. These sketches look an awful lot like you, man. I figured you might want to know. Enough said. Good luck, and we never talked, you understand?"

"Thanks, pal, you never called," Jackson said, and hung up.

He knew from the first hit on Baby Junior that they'd be coming for him, but he thought he'd have more time. An icy hand gripped his heart, then a hint of momentary panic. But he quickly shook it off, knowing he wasn't running. No way. He was compelled to finish what he'd started and take out the Wolfpack shot-caller directly responsible for authorizing Arlette's murder, regardless of the personal consequences. It would be wise to make himself hard to find in The City.

Jackson tossed the rest of the pizza in the garbage, went into the bedroom, and quickly packed an overnight bag with stuff he'd need, including the .357 automatic. He had a pair of good follow-up leads on the whereabouts of Breed to check out tonight. Then he'd hole up in a cheap motel until he was ready to plan out a move on the shot-caller.

The beginning of the end for him was nearing, and it would undoubtedly end badly. So be it. He'd vowed to Arlette in ICU before she died that he'd revenge her senseless shooting.

And thinking about the three previous hits, including the young woman, he felt no lingering sense of remorse. No trouble sleeping. But, as a cop, and still subscribing to the social importance of the rule of law, he knew he also had to face the legal consequences of his vigilante executions. After putting Breed down, he'd turn himself in to the homicide division of SFPD.

He took off in the old Escort, headed for the Bay Bridge.

FIVE

Revenge is an act of passion; vengeance of justice. Injuries are revenged; crimes are avenged.

—Samuel Johnson

All four investigators were gathered together at the P.I. office to plan strategy, now that they knew their suspect's name. Harlan had dug up Jackson's Oakland address from personnel and had checked it against a current DMV address. He was living near Lake Merritt in a duplex apartment. He'd checked with Oakland PD and found that Jackson was currently a Detective Sergeant in the narcotics division, but had been off duty for over thirty-five days, having taken almost all his accumulated vacation time in one lump.

Johnny opened the meeting after writing a few items on the progress board, including the legal name and background Hap had uncovered from the *old* shot-caller for the *current* shot-caller, Breed, AKA Aldon Manspeaker.

He was an atypical shot-caller, and, apparently, a bit of a recluse, never hanging around the usual gang locations. Even though the Wolfpack was into selling dope, Manspeaker worked a regular job at his aunt's bakery, Donuts Plus, near Hunter's Point. He began work at three in morning, finishing by nine, six days a week, and lived in a small apartment over the bakery. All this information about the shot-caller of the Wolfpack was quickly written on the progress board, and then momentarily pushed aside.

They were focused now on the cop responsible for the recent murders of the two Wolfpack gangbangers and their driver.

"Okay," Johnny said. "We need to check out Jackson's place in Oakland, talk to the neighbors, do some surveillance before we even consider getting the Oakland Swat team stirred up to take Jackson down. We need to move on him quickly. He could be running."

"I don't think he'll run," Katy said. "As a veteran cop, he must know he's living on borrowed time since shooting Baby Jr. I agree we need to take him soon, but without rushing and making poor decisions just for the sake of expediency. No question Jackson knows how to handle a gun and will use it. He's dangerous."

After a pause, everyone agreed Katy's suggested course of action made the safest and best sense.

The four checked out a duplex apartment near Lake Merritt the next day. With no one coming or going, they split up and interviewed the closest neighbors. Jackson had indeed taken an extended vacation, but in the last month he'd apparently never left town, and was in and out of his apartment at all hours, day and night.

The investigators figured he'd used that time conducting his own private investigation to locate, then stalk, and finally hit the Qwik Mart shooters and the driver. The four decided to begin a surveillance of his apartment that afternoon.

There were no indications of Jackson being at home, though. When they'd asked around the immediate neighborhood, the nearest neighbors knew him to be a very private man, no girlfriends or any other visitors in the late evenings. The only exception had been several months ago when his daughter had visited and stayed in the apartment. She'd only stayed a few days. During that time, they'd taken long walks every morning around nearby Lake Merritt, the daughter often able to bring a smile to Jackson's face. But that young woman had been gone for several months, Jackson all alone.

At about eight-thirty, after Johnny and Katy had setup in their car across the street from the duplex, lights remained off in Jackson's half.

"He may be out for dinner," Katy said.

"*Hmmm*, or he goes to be bed really early," Johnny said half-joking, then glanced at his watch. "Nah, even on vacation time, he'd be accustomed to keeping late hours from his work habits for all the years working narcotics. Who knows where the dude is now. He's probably burnt up most of his time off, though, chasing everyone down. He'll need to return to work soon. Whatever he's doing, he needs to finish it up quickly."

"Maybe he's busy looking for Breed, the one he probably feels is ultimately responsible for his daughter's death." Katy nodded, as if agreeing with herself.

They waited on the stakeout until after midnight with no luck spotting Jackson.

All four investigators met the next morning early at the P.I. office. After some discussion, they finally agreed with Katy that Jackson was probably planning on taking out the Wolfpack shot-caller, since Breed was ultimately responsible for authorizing the shootings that resulted in his daughter's death. And, by now, he had probably dug up the man's real name and location.

They decided they would shift their major surveillance efforts to Hunter's Point, the Donuts Plus bakery, and Aldon Manspeaker's overhead apartment, and to randomly check back on the Lake Merritt duplex in Oakland if necessary. One of the closest neighbors, a homebody, agreed to call Harlan if she saw Jackson at his apartment. But they were pretty sure now that Jackson wasn't returning there.

Hap mentioned there was a possibility that Jackson might've been alerted by a cop friend that he was now being hunted.

The four agreed on beginning an early morning surveillance on the bakery. Jackson would know Manspeaker's schedule by now, his routine, and would probably attempt to hit the shot-caller on his way to work. An alley ran behind the bakery, with a tall cyclone fence separating it from the backside of a multi-storied apartment complex. No one would be around in the alley so early in the morning, and Manspeaker might not be the most alert at that hour.

The perfect situation for a hit.

Katy contributed most of this analysis, and the others agreed with her.

They arrived earlier, at two-thirty a.m., and parked in a small parking lot that served several businesses fronting the main drag, 3rd street, which included a laundry, a beauty parlor, a pizza joint, and Donuts Plus. All were armed with handguns.

Johnny and Katy hid behind a double stack of collapsed cardboard boxes directly across the alley and facing the bakery's back door. With their backs resting against the cyclone fencing, there was nothing near them except the large blue dumpster about a hundred feet away.

Hap and Harlan were out of sight at the far southern end of the alley. They'd decided Jackson would appear from that southerly direction, a direct path from the small parking lot on 3rd, and figured he would be able to get in and out quickest from that direction. And at that time, there would be no worry about witnesses.

2.

Katy and Johnny squatted and waited as fog thickened around them. The damp chill gave Katy goosebumps, time seeming to stall. She checked her watch every five minutes. The dumpster smelled of rotted food, making her nose itch—the reason they'd avoided hiding back there.

Around two fifty-five, the door at the top of the steps over the bakery popped open. Manspeaker looked out, surveyed the alley, and then emerged from his apartment, walking quickly down the steps. He paused at the bakery back door, fumbling for a key.

As the gangbanger stood under the light over the door, a figure stepped out from the darkness behind the dumpster and assumed a combat shooter's stance—

"Drop down, Aldon!" Katy shouted.

Aldon reacted instantly, dropping to his knees as the dark figure dashed into the outer circle of better light and fired.

Ping.

The round hit midway up the bakery door, barely missing the kneeling man. Manspeaker quickly unlocked and pulled open the door and scrambled inside, out of sight.

Johnny and Katy moved out from their hiding spot with their automatics drawn and stood in the middle of the alley, blocking the shooter.

"Hold it, Jackson," Johnny shouted, "drop your—"

Ping.

The round buzzed high over Katy's head.

Instinctively, she'd dropped forward slightly into her shooter's stance, aimed, and squeezed off a round from her 9mm automatic.

Bang.

Jackson went down, clutching high on his right thigh.

Running footsteps thundered in the fog from the alley behind them. In a full sprint, Hap darted by, knelt over the fallen and moaning Jackson, and quickly disarmed him.

Johnny checked on Manspeaker inside the bakery, not hit, but shaken up.

Harlan called an ambulance and alerted Homicide.

The four investigators quickly gathered around. In spite of Jackson's injury, Hap had cuffed the shooter's hands tightly behind his back.

"*Ohhhh,*" Jackson moaned under his breath, the side of his face planted against the wet alley asphalt.

Katy pulled a handkerchief from her pocket.

"Lie still," she ordered, as she pressed the cloth tightly against his bloody thigh. She glanced up. "Everyone give me your hankies, maybe we can slow this bleeding until the EMTs get here." In the background, sirens wailed, getting louder.

Harlan went around to 3rd Street to guide them to the alley.

Minutes later, Jackson was transported to Kaiser Hospital in South San Francisco.

The crew remained for three hours at the shooting site, Harlan explaining what had happened to the first responding uniform cops; then later as he was questioned by homicide detectives. What had they been doing out there at that time of morning? Why?

Later he answered to an angry homicide lieutenant's numerous questions, including why he was accompanied by three armed civilians, despite their approved consulting status, and why they were physically involved in taking down a suspect on a Homicide case, and why Harlan hadn't called for proper backup?

Katy, Johnny, and Hap were repeatedly questioned, too. They were finally free to go at about six-thirty in the morning.

After the Internal Affairs Department finished grilling Harlan later on that same morning, Katy figured he'd be lucky to not be fired or suspended in a few days when their report and recommendations were finished and filed, despite the fact that they'd caught the rogue cop. The next day the *Chronicle* anointed Harlan, and his consulting P.I.s, *hero status*. And remarkably, by default, Harlan remained assigned to the case awaiting the IAD recommendations.

Later that same evening, Harlan and Katy were waiting at Kaiser Hospital ICU, and visited Jackson after he came out of surgery on his thigh. Lucky for him, the round had not hit a major artery, and barely nicked his femur. But he had a guard outside his door and was cuffed to the bed, even though he wouldn't be walking any time soon.

Harlan pulled out a recorder and began his Miranda Rights Statement: "You have the right to remain silent—"

Jackson waved it off and said, "Cut. I'll sign that I understand my legal rights. What do you want to know?"

Harlan finished the Miranda Statement anyhow, then pointed at the recorder, and asked if Jackson understood and agreed to being recorded.

"Yes, I understand my rights and agree to you recording my statements."

Katy said, "Why did you shoot at Johnny and me after you missed hitting Manspeaker at the bakery door?"

"I fired high, thinking you'd both duck for cover. I wasn't trying to hit either of you, and thought I could trap Manspeaker inside the bakery. I didn't know about the two other detectives, until they appeared running up the alley toward us."

Katy nodded.

Harlan said, "But you had to realize it was over for you, even if you'd managed to kill Manspeaker."

Jackson pointed at Katy and said, "Half an hour earlier I saw you and your partner hiding behind the stack of cardboard. So, I knew I'd be immediately taken into custody. But first, I wanted an opportunity to take out the shot-caller responsible for Arlette's murder, at any cost."

"He would've been the last of the four you determined were directly involved in your daughter's death, right?" Harlan asked.

"Yes, even if you hadn't been there in the alley, after getting Manspeaker, I planned on turning myself in."

A stern-faced nurse came into the room, interrupting. "Wrap it up, please. Mr. Jackson needs his rest."

Harlan turned to him and asked, "You are willing to sign a complete confession to three murders and an attempted murder?"

Jackson nodded.

"I'll ask for your word that you'll sign the confession when I get it printed up and return."

"Okay, I'll sign that when you get it."

Harlan added, "And before we leave, Katy has one more question she'd like to ask."

"Ask away, young lady."

"It's actually a two-part question," Katy said. "Did you place a wrapped stick of Doublemint gum in each of your victim's left hands after shooting them? And, if so, *why?*"

Again, Jackson nodded. "I'm pretty sure Arlette was reaching in her purse for a stick of Doublemint gum just before she was hit. She always had a pack with her. Her favorite flavor. Chewed it whenever she was nervous. But she never had the opportunity to unwrap that stick of gum. I thought it fitting that each of the three killers would *never* unwrap theirs either. Tonight, I had one stick left for Aldon Manspeaker."

Later that night, Katy and Johnny returned home to their apartment, got a couple of Henrys out of the fridge, sat at the kitchen table, and let out a collective sigh. They both had a warm glow in their chests, which they always felt after solving a case and finally tying up all the loose ends. Tomorrow night they planned on meeting with Harlan and Hap at the P.I. office for a mini-celebration, Harlan buying and bringing the pizza and beer. After that, it would take another day or two for Katy to come down, pull herself together mentally, and get committed to writer mode again. She planned a full court press on The White Plague Chronicles.

SIX

Integrity has no need of rules.

—Albert Camus

The next night, Harlan was late for the victory celebration. While they waited, Katy looked over the progress board, which they hadn't bothered to erase, even though the case was solved. Johnny would usually take a photo of the board for the file before erasing. She reread every entry again, because she still felt there was something important to the case she just wasn't quite able to pinpoint. Nothing was popping out to her, but she couldn't let it go.

At that moment, Johnny's cell phone rang. He answered and a moment later grimaced and said, "No shit, that just can't *be*!" He listened with a kind of shocked disbelief etched into his expression for a full minute or two more, and then finally thumbed off his cell phone.

"That was Harlan," he said, making a deep sigh, but still wearing the stunned look and shaking his head in disbelief. "Manspeaker was shot in his apartment above the bakery about an hour ago. Harlan said he was calling on his way over to the murder scene. But here's the unbelievable part: The first responding uniform cop said he found a wrapped stick of Doublemint gum in Manspeaker's hand… "

No one commented. All three sat stone silent.

How could this be? Katy thought. *Unless Jackson was loose from the hospital and could walk well enough to take down Manspeaker, which seemed impossible—*

Johnny interrupted her thought. "Harlan wants us to split up and quickly check out what has to be the major suspect and other persons of interest. Hap, go see Jackson at the hospital, if he's still there. Katy and I will go to the James place and talk to them. Okay let's roll, folks. We'll meet back here at the office to exchange results with Harlan as soon as possible."

Mrs. James let them in, not really looking too unhappy to see them. She had probably already been informed about Kenneth Jackson being responsible for shooting the two gangbangers and their driver. And that he was currently in custody.

As Katy repeated this information, Mrs. James wore a resigned expression. She responded in a sad voice. "Well, it doesn't bring Arlette back, and now Kenny is in the biggest trouble of his life."

"Mrs. James," Johnny said, "were you at home all evening? And I'm guessing Mr. James must be still at work?"

"I've been here all night visiting with two girlfriends, who just left minutes ago; and Tony was here in his study working most of the evening, too. But, he had to leave maybe ten minutes ago for the office to attend a video conference with their New York office, and their overseas IPO client."

There was really nothing more to talk about. The answer was obviously easy enough for them to check out and validate their alibis.

Johnny rubbed his nose.

"Thank you, Mrs. James," Katy said, as she stood to leave. "We appreciate your time and cooperation."

In the car, riding back from the James home, Katy was reminded of something important on the progress board, and suspected it might be buried in the James information under the MISC. DATA heading. Possibly something she *should* have asked Mrs. James tonight? Katy couldn't recall what that might have been. She'd check it out when they got back to the office.

2.

Johnny and Katy were the last getting back to the P.I. office. Harlan and Hap were waiting for their return and report.

Johnny said, "Both Mr. and Mrs. James's whereabouts tonight are easily accounted for. Neither could've hit Manspeaker. What did you guys find out?"

"When I got to the hospital," Hap said, "Kenneth Jackson was fast asleep, full of medication, still cuffed to his bed. I woke him, waited for him to shake out the mental cobwebs, then told him about the Manspeaker hit and the gum. He just smiled and nodded, but didn't, or *wouldn't*, say if he knew anything about the hit. I pressed him about having a partner, but Jackson wouldn't budge, just shrugged and didn't respond at all."

Johnny pointed at Harlan. "What's up at the scene?"

"The shooter must have been invited into Manspeaker's apartment. There were no signs of a break-in, or any kind of scuffle in the apartment. Looks to me like someone just casually walked in and shot him in the face; then, they picked up the shell casing, placed a stick of Doublemint into the victim's hand, and walked out. They left no other clues. If you all want to go over and take a look at the scene—"

"Better not," Johnny said. "We've already stirred up enough trouble for you with Internal Affairs."

It was quiet for a few minutes, no one having anything else to say.

Katy realized that like her, they were all puzzled by the unexpected execution, and especially by the stick of *Doublemint*.

Who else knew about the gum in the other victims' hands?

She figured the other detectives were mulling over the same thoughts.

Katy remembered to check the MISC. DATA column. Her gaze slowly moved halfway down the notes. She stopped at a question she'd written in parentheses after their notes on the results of that first interview with Mrs. James: *Why was Arlette's sister, Annette, estranged from the family?* The question had never been answered.

Why indeed? Katy asked herself. *Did it have any bearing on the case, or this newest turn of events?* It could, but she wasn't sure. Katy glanced at her watch. It was not too late to call Mrs. James and ask—despite the touchy nature of the family relationships—and hope for an answer.

"Mrs. James? Katy Green here. Sorry to bother you again so soon. One more question or two, please. Why was Arlette's sister estranged from the family? And where is Annette now?"

There was such a long pause that Katy was afraid Mrs. James was not going to answer either question.

Then, finally, a dry cough, the voice being cleared. "Annette began visiting her blood father, Kenneth Jackson, over in Oakland when she was a senior in high school, despite Tony and I absolutely forbidding it. After a series of arguments, she finally left home, just a few days before graduation. We think she stayed here in The City with a close friend's family until she graduated from high school. I suspected that she and Arlette continued to see each other and communicate regularly, because, as twins, they'd always been so close. But her name was never mentioned again in our home. I don't have any idea where Annette might be now."

After a few moments of silence, Katy said, "Thank you Mrs. James," and hung up.

It wasn't Arlette visiting her dad a couple months ago. It had *to have been Annette…*

The light bulb went on over her head. *With her dad out of commission, Annette* has *to be the prime suspect in Manspeaker's shooting.*

Katy spelled this conclusion out to the other detectives.

"Okay," Johnny said, "no question that we need to find Annette. And we need to do it quickly, before she flees, if she hasn't done that already."

The next morning, Harlan, after a number of phone calls, had discovered where Annette James had been the last few months after last visiting her dad in Oakland. She'd joined the Marines. And had apparently done well in fourteen weeks of boot camp at MCRD in San Diego, and another three more weeks of Infantry Training Regiment at Camp Pendleton. But three days ago, she had checked out from Camp Pendleton on leave in San Francisco, with orders to report for flight school at the Naval Air Station in Pensacola, Florida, this week.

"Okay," Johnny said, rubbing his nose, "she came home. She might still be here."

"But we know she isn't staying at her dad's apartment," Hap said, frowning slightly, "or at the James's place, either. Where would she be staying?"

After a few moments thought, Katy suggested in a tentative voice, "I wonder if she has a Marine buddy also calling this area home. Maybe an old high school friend. Maybe she's staying at that friend's family place."

"Good thinking, Katy," Johnny said. "But what's the best way to check that out?"

"Well," Katy said after holding up a forefinger, "maybe Chandler, Arlette's boyfriend, can help. He probably knows all the twins' high school friends."

"Let's give him another visit," Johnny said, getting up, with a thin grin on his face.

3.

They were lucky. Chandler was at his apartment studying for a late afternoon exam. He invited them in and asked them to sit around a small dining room table.

"We'll make this brief, Chandler," Johnny said, nodding at the papers and books laid out on the kitchen table, "and let you get back to studying. This is part of the routine investigation to all these gangbanger murders, and specifically the most recent murder of the Wolfpack's shot-caller. We're interested in the circle of friends Arlette and Annette shared in their last year in high school. A specific friend, one who Annette *may* have lived with before graduating, after she was banned from the James's home. Can you help us out here?'

Chandler grinned broadly, nodding. "That's easy. Annette stayed with her best friend—Eileen Gray—at her grandmother's apartment on Divisidero Street. When her dad got promoted and transferred from work to Houston, Eileen stayed and moved down there from Pacific Heights so she could finish her last few months at Lowell High School."

Katy asked, "Can you tell us about Eileen and Annette's relationship, more recently?"

"Well, let's see. Arlette, Annette, and Eileen were all volunteers at Kaiser Hospital their last two years, and then after graduating, Annette and Eileen stayed on as full-time paid aides, and continued to live with Eileen's grandmother." Chandler rubbed his chin in thought. "I remember Arlette mentioned that both the girls quit Kaiser three or four months ago to join the Marine Corps, of all things." He shrugged, lifted his eyebrows. "Arlette thought both girls wanted to qualify for the Naval Flight School in Florida and be fighter pilots. Unusual aspiration for these two super-bright girls, in my opinion. Annette was always the most adventuresome of the twins. So, we should have suspected something like that from her."

"That's all very helpful," Katy said, smiling. "Have you seen Annette and Eileen around more recently, like maybe after Arlette died?"

Chandler shook his head.

Johnny gave him his P.I. card. "Well, if you hear from either of them, call me, okay?"

"I will," the young man said, putting the card in his wallet.

"We'll let you get back to your studies," Johnny said, "and thanks."

4.

Harlan phoned his previous contact at Marine Corps records. The contact phoned back in ten minutes. Harlan hung up, grinned, and nodded. "Yes, Eileen Gray went through the same platoon in boot camp with Annette, and both graduated from ITR together. They checked out on leave at the same time, with Eileen having orders to join Annette for flight training in Pensacola, Florida. Both are due to report to that naval air base in no later than six days."

"Okay," Johnny said, "we need to visit Grandma. I'm hoping they're still there."

"Right," Harlan agreed. "And let's do it *now*. No time to wait for back-up."

The four investigators left to check out the apartment on Divisidero Street. They parked near the two-story building, which had four separate units. They decided Hap and Harlan would go in the front door. Katy and Johnny would go around back and watch, just in case Annette was actually in there and decided to run.

There was a set of steps down from the upper two apartments, which led to a wide porch that also served the downstairs units. Behind the porch were four parking spaces for cars—three empty—with an older Honda Accord parked in the fourth space.

"Are you in place," Harlan asked Johnny on his cell phone.

"Yes."

"Okay, get ready to tango."

Johnny and Katy listened anxiously for gun shots…

Nothing but silence from Grandma's apartment—

Then the back door exploded open, and Johnny was knocked off the porch by a charging blur—a massive, tan pit bull, the dog locking down on Johnny's right arm. Running in the wake of the fierce dog was a tall, young woman.

Katy kicked the pit bull in the head, but the dog didn't release her partner. She had to draw her handgun and shoot it. She turned toward Annette, who had paused near the Honda, looking back over her shoulder after hearing the shot.

Katy assumed a shooter's crouch and shouted, "That's it, Annette! It's over."

The athletic-looking young woman, in series of practiced moves, quickly hopped side to side, and dropped into a kneeling position, elbow on her knee, sighting a handgun.

Bang!

Katy was hit in her left shoulder before she could get off a round. She was driven backward, falling off-balance onto her side on the porch.

Bang!

Johnny, in the prone position, fired at Annette, despite his chewed-up arm bleeding badly. He hit the young woman in the chest. Her weapon flew out of her hand as she fell.

Hap and Harlan came out the back door and crouched with their guns drawn, but the shooting was over.

Time to call for medical help… and for Harlan to alert Homicide.

Johnny said he was fine. Katy said that she was okay and that the guys should see what they could do for Annette.

Hap administered first aid to the groaning young woman as best he could, but he couldn't stop the bleeding. He said that he suspected a major artery had been hit.

The young woman lay on her back, her eyes teared-up and blinking rapidly. She was finally able to keep her eyes open long enough to speak in a hoarse whisper. "Arlette was going to be a doctor. I was going to be a fighter pilot, but now… "

Her voice trailed off as she made an odd circling motion with her forefinger in the palm of her opposite hand.

5.

You say: "We began together, now we will end together. I'm coming, sister."

EPILOGUE

Katy and Johnny were both temporarily hospitalized. Johnny stayed only a few hours to get his dog bite wound cleaned, and a hair-line fracture of his right radius casted. Katy had only a flesh wound in her shoulder from the shot, no bones, arteries, or organs hit. She was released a day later from the hospital.

Harlan Bundy was not fired, but suspended for two weeks without pay after the IAD reports were submitted. He eventually returned to his Homicide unit better respected for clearing up four homicides, even though he used out-of-the-box methods and civilian personnel.

After write-ups in the *Chronicle*, Johnny and Hap's private investigator agency experienced a big uptick in investigation requests.

Katy returned to her writing, experiencing good critical and commercial success when the two-book series, The White Plague Chronicles, was published. The first book, *The Sarawak Virus*, received a starred review in *Publishers Weekly*, and made *The New York Times* bestseller list.

And so, the case of the San Francisco vigilante executions began to fade into memories.

The End

… and don't miss out on the other thrilling books in this series:

The Crime Files of Katy Green #1: Double Jack

The Crime Files of Katy Green #2: Shadow of the Dark Angel

The Crime Files of Katy Green #3: Deathflash

The Crime Files of Katy Green #4: A Stick of Doublemint

Truth and the Common Man:

A Series Afterword of Sorts

by Gord Rollo

Anyone up for a quick chat about Sherlock Holmes?

No, wait… stay with me for a minute. No need to double-check the book cover. We're all in the right place. I'm well aware that I'm here to talk to you about Gene O'Neill and his terrific series collectively dubbed *The Crime Files of Katy Green*, and I'll get there—promise, but bear with me for just a moment. You see, whenever I pick up a stand-alone detective book, or a series of books as in this case, my mind drifts back to all the great fictional detectives and private investigators of the past. You can't help but do the comparison thing, right? And my guess is everyone who reads this will have heard of good old Sherlock.

You can substitute any other great detective you've enjoyed reading over the years (Hercule Poirot, Sam Spade, Philip Marlowe, Miss Marple, Spenser, Matthew Scudder, Harry Bosch, Lucas Davenport, Charlie Parker) into this discussion too, because at their heart—and this is the point I want to get at—they all have the *exact* same job description. Regardless of who you want to focus on, if you boil down their make-believe resumes to their most basic skill, they all do the same thing: Detectives look for the truth. That's it… that's all. Period.

I'm no expert on Sir Arthur Conan Doyle's fiction, but I've read a fair amount of it and still get a rush when I hear Holmes shouting at his trusty sidekick Watson to "*Hurry up, the game is afoot…* " Holmes doesn't say it in every adventure, but he says it in a great many of them, and it is often spoken at a critical moment in the ever-thickening plot where tension is at its highest, and Holmes is close to figuring everything out. He's on the move, on the chase, and he's loving every second of the hunt for the answer at the end of the mystery. Because that's what Holmes lives for—the challenge and, more importantly, the truth. When everything else is stripped away, boys and girls, the truth is what all great fiction *should* be about.

I'm pretty sure you have all read or heard the famous line, "*When you have eliminated the impossible, whatever remains, however improbable, must be the truth.*" Believe it or not, Holmes says this line, or a close variation of it in over half a dozen different adventures. As he should, because it's a kick-ass line, and it helps bring us back to what we came here to talk about. The truth doesn't just refer to whether a character is telling lies or not. It's not just that a writer should get his facts straight and do his research about the people and places he or she is writing about. The truth for a writer (and by extension the people reading their work), means so much more than that.

So let's talk about Gene now.

Although I have no way of knowing, my guess is that most of you reading this are already fans of Gene's work on one level or another and have read various pieces of his *Cal Wild* tales, or some of his award-winning short stories. That's good. Really good. Nice to know there are still lots of readers out there with refined taste in literature. The question becomes then, why do we like Gene's fiction so much? What is it about his stories that resonate within us and keep us coming back? Maybe some would accuse me of being a bit too much of a friend and fanboy, but to hell with it; it's my honest opinion that Gene's body of work ranks up among the true masters of speculative fiction and stands shoulder to shoulder with any fiction produced by greats like Dickens, Tolkien, Hammett, Chandler, Asimov, Matheson, King, and Bradbury. Feel free to substitute or add in any other writer you feel should be on that list, and I'm obviously not just including mystery, fantasy, and detective novelists—I'm talking about the whole canon of fiction here. The names aren't as important to me as the elements that their timeless fictions have in common, and we need to take a closer look at that next.

Read back the list of writers I just mentioned. When you think about what things in common their stories and books all share, what do you come up with? Me, I see a list of writers that regardless of timeframes or genres or where their work might be placed by critics on the literate/entertainment scale, they all overwhelmingly preferred to write about the truth in our daily lives. About the good, the bad, and the downright nasty parts of life, sure, but always about the truth their characters' lives are based on. Their joys, their sorrows, their triumphs, and most definitely their struggles. In other words, they wrote about the collective *us*. That means you and me. Toss our family, friends, neighbors, and co-workers in there too. Some villains and bad guys too obviously, because every great story need some of those. They wrote about everyday people trying their best to get through one day to the next and about how even the smallest and weakest of us can rise above our situations and become something great. Or at least try to, right? Things don't always work out as planned, but that too is just like the real lives you and I lead every day. We all have hopes and dreams and grand plans that we strive to accomplish. Some of us will succeed. Some will fail. Some will be winners. Some won't, but the key element gluing everything together is the struggle that we all go through to *try* and make it. The very best literature out there zeroes in on that simple truth and to me, at least, it is that binding element in their fiction that makes that list of writers I mentioned rise above the millions of writers trying to emulate their successes.

Truth and the common man.

Or common woman too, naturally—Katy Green would kick my ass if I didn't include her and other great female detectives into this discussion—but that's what it's all about, kids. It's what everyone wants to read about. It's what we *need* to read about, if we are going to buy in and invest our souls in the characters. Cut all the bullshit out and just hit us with the truth, brother. We're already fully aware that life isn't always fair, and that people aren't always perfect. We all have flaws. People constantly fail. They make mistakes. They do stupid things. It's not always easy to do, but in the end we keep trying... we pick our sorry asses up off the turf and keep moving forward. And that's what I think people want to read about in their fiction.

Why? Because it's real.

Real people. Real problems. Real Life.

Gene O'Neill's number one strength as an author is that he writes about this daily struggle as well, and it's that fact, that brilliant unwavering truth in his words that catches and holds our attention. No matter if he is telling us a story set in today's real world or some wild far-future tales, the truth about real people—about you and me—shines through.

I've asked him about this key element in his writing before, back in 2004 when I was an editor for a small press called Prime Books. I was putting together a collection of Gene's short stories and asked him to write me an afterword to that book explaining why he wrote and why this daily struggle, or *The Grand Struggle* as he called it, for life influenced his fiction so much. I could recap what he said for you here but seeing as that book is long out of print and hardly any of you will have read it, I'd like to reprint it for you in its entirety. It speaks so perfectly to what I've been discussing and will give you a wonderful glimpse into how Gene sees the world and how it's the everyday experiences in life that shape his creative process.

You're going to love this...

———

Question: What do you write about, Gene? Why?

Short answer: I write about *loss*, because it interests me.

Detailed answer: I grew up in the fifties on the West Coast near the shadows of shipyard cranes in a federally subsidized housing project. My people were the working class/poor. Most of the significant things

I know I learned during that time. Perhaps more importantly, even though I wasn't aware of the process, it was during these early years I honed my writerly sensibilities.

I learned to compete in most of the major sports at the local Recreation Center, loved them all, but especially contact sports like boxing and basketball—oh yeah, basketball like we played was a full contact sport. From boxing I learned something about honor, integrity, and courage—and the only friend you have in the ring is a clinch. From basketball I learned something about discipline and hard work—and scoring isn't everything. At the Rec, I learned that with perseverance and heart, one could accomplish a great deal. At this time, jocks, especially in high school and those who made it to college, were much admired—they were exempt from most of the bullying and petty racism. Of course I realized at some point that sports would not be a career for me (although I played college basketball and taught P.E.). Remarkably, I competed at the Rec with at least twenty guys who went on to play college ball, and four who became professional baseball or football players.

During those early years, I was exposed to violence, sex, crime, racism, and a kind of ghetto code of ethics—you stand up for yourself, no matter the number and size of the enemy; you never give up a friend to anyone in authority; you haul your own trash, never requesting assistance from teachers, parents, or the law; and you have a suspicion of anyone who says that they have only your best interests at heart. This code was rigidly practiced at school, on the street, and at the Rec.

Most importantly I learned to pay attention to things going on around me. I soon realized that most folks, sooner or later, dealt with some kind of loss in their life. Loss of a loved one—grandparent, parent, sibling, children—claimed by disease, accident, murder, or by their own hand. Loss of a job—layoff, fired, quit, or the job just disappeared. Some of the loss I didn't notice until I grew older because it happened slowly, was harder to spot. Loss of self-respect. Loss of dignity. Loss of trust. Loss of feeling—caring. Often one loss was subtly added to another—the loss of self-respect accompanied loss of a job; the loss of dignity sometimes followed a series of losses. In one way or another, every man, woman, and child I knew was forced to deal with the pain of loss. Most adjusted and carried on.

As I learned later on, struggling with loss isn't unique to the working class/ poor. No indeed, the middle class, the rich cope, too. But it's different. When a Harvard-trained lawyer leaves a Wall Street firm, it isn't devastating. He has many options. When flange turners were no longer needed at shipyards, highly skilled craftsmen found themselves stripped of status—it was too late to retrain as machinists, they were flange turners. When a baby delays the completion of a parent's MBA at Stanford, it's not quite so earthshaking as a pregnant fourteen-year-old dropping out of Chabot Junior High School.

Looking back it is evident that those working class/poor, dealt with a disproportionate/more serious share of loss. A large number never finished high school, many spent time in jail, some graduated to prison, and a few found themselves on death row at San Quentin. Single mothers were common—sometimes with a series of "uncles" sharing the rent. Drugs, alcohol, gambling, abuse, all commonplace. These things touched most of the families I knew. But despite the difficulties, I never saw people as good or evil. They were just people making choices. Sometimes the choices demonstrated poor judgment, and bad situations could develop. Even now I vividly remember the constant battle against heavy odds, people struggling with devastating loss, but coping, attempting to overcome high hurdles, adjusting to tremendous pain, and even aspiring to something better for themselves and especially for their children.

All this I think of as *The Grand Struggle*.

This is what I write about. Not heroes or villains. Just people. Real people attempting to survive, doing their best despite the odds.

Win or lose, it is the struggle that remains fascinating.

———

There you have it, folks. Straight from the horse's… I mean, Gene's mouth. Do you see where it cuts through all the crap and just tells it like it is? It's an essay about people. About life, love, triumph, tragedy, joy, and sorrow as much as it is about writing and that, to me, is what makes Gene's fiction so incredibly powerful. It's the real deal, you know? In this age where bullshit rules supreme, a writer who can clear the windshield of life and show you the truth while you're along for the ride will always stand above the average writer who tries to force you to see his or her blurred version of the world. The truth always shines through in the end, and we, as average common people, have an ear for that and appreciate the honesty.

Gene O'Neill writes about you and me, my friends. He writes about our hopes and dreams, about our loves and losses, and although there are rarely any happy Hollywood endings in his tales, Gene has an uncanny ability to show us the good inside people, to show us the potential we all carry within us as human beings. The stories you have read in this excellent series are perfect examples of this. *Double Jack*, *Shadow of the Dark Angel, Deathflash*, and *A Stick of Doublemint* will talk to your heart about love and loss and, yes, *The Grand Struggle* of everyday life on the streets. There's obviously a lot of rape, murder, revenge, and other nasty stuff happening in those crime stories too, but violence is a harsh reality in our world and to shy away from it or fluff it into something less horrible than what it truly is would be to flinch, and an author should never flinch. An author has to be able to look evil straight in the eye and report exactly what they see or else they're cheating their readers out of the truth—and the reader will always know. Always.

Gene taught me that.

Katy Green isn't a hero. She's a regular person. Just an everyday woman trying to do her job. She doesn't have super powers or possess the ability to read minds. She just does her job and methodically goes about doing what all great fictional detectives do: she searches for the truth until she finds it—or it finds her. Just like Sherlock Holmes and Hercule Poirot did. Just like Sam Spade and Philip Marlowe. Like Lucas Davenport and Harry Bosch. Perhaps even like regular Joes such as you and I would too if we were ever in her shoes. Not heroes even on our best day, but if fate smiled on us, hopefully we all have some heroic qualities inside of us that would surface when we needed them most.

The cool part to me is that Gene can subtly reveal the enduring spirit that makes us all capable of being heroes but does it without beating you over the head with any heavy-handed sermons. Gene's fiction, like his characters, have a way of sneaking up on you. The truth and the moral lessons lie buried within their stories, subtly working their magic on you as you are pulled along for the ride. And as readers, what more could we ever ask for than that?

Let me leave you with one more juicy tidbit for you to chew on as you close this book. The ride may not be over. Katy Green may not be settling into retirement and her full-time writing career quite yet. I've heard a strange rumor that is going around in the great state of California these days. Murmurs that I think started quietly on Death Row in San Quentin Maximum Security Penitentiary but have begun to spread throughout the prison and to the outside through those "in the know." Fearful whispers passed from cell to cell, inmate to inmate. Rumors of an escape plan perhaps already being set in motion by one of their biggest and baddest residents; a fiendish four hundred-pound serial killer with an axe to grind with the detectives who put him there. Cato and the Green Hornet may have to ride again someday. They may not have any choice.

Then again… it could be just a rumor.

Gord Rollo
February 22, 2020
Great White North

Gord Rollo was born in St. Andrews, Scotland, but now lives in Ontario, Canada. His short stories and novella-length work have appeared in many professional publications throughout the genre and his novels include: *The Jigsaw Man, Crimson, Strange Magic, Valley of the Scarecrow,* and *The Translators.* His work has been translated into several languages and his titles are currently being adapted for audiobooks.

Bonus! Interview with Author Gene O'Neill, Conducted by B.E. Scully

B.E. Scully: Hi Gene, and thanks for taking some time to speak with me. I've been a longtime fan of your work, and have enjoyed all of the volumes of the Katy Green detective series. My personal favorite was the third volume, *Deathflash*. To some, young Billy Williams might seem like the kind of anti-hero our cities "need" right now. What went into your conception of the character? Did you have his fate planned out beforehand or did he evolve as you wrote?

Gene O' Neil: I think I was in the Marine Corps when I first asked myself: *And then what?* The question was generated by the question of dying and death. An early interest. So, fifteen or maybe more years ago, I came across the translation of a Russian experiment. They were taking a kind of photograph over the body of persons dying. Similar to

Kirilian Photography. But the Russians were interested in the amount of radiation the body released at the moment of death. Surprisingly, experiment after experiment came up with the same result: The body released one hundred times the amount of radiation normally contained in a living body at death. Wow! What was this flash? The obvious answer for a religious person would be: the soul departing. I was never able to validate duplication of this experiment here in the U.S. for obviously ethical reasons. So, I filed it away, thinking I'd do a short story along these lines, even using the title, *Deathflash*. I did a first draft of a religious commune based on the leader being able to see that "death flash." But it never went anywhere until I developed another theme utilizing another image of it: a heroin overdose. That book was eventually developed answering some of the stats and questions in the next question here.

BES: According to recent statistics, more than 90,000 people died from opioid overdoses in the USA in the years 2016 and 2017 combined, and more than 135,000 died from all drug overdoses in those two years. Both are higher than the 58,220 USA service member deaths in Vietnam. You've included themes and characters involving drug addiction and the drug trade in your work many times throughout your career, but perhaps in no more profound and probing way than in *Deathflash*. Tell us a bit about your history with this subject, and how your perspective has or has not changed throughout the decades.

GON: I found similar statistics as those reflected in your question deeply disturbing. Because my family has the Irish curse of a susceptibility to alcohol/drug abuse. My son, Gavin, as a teen interested in music—especially punk rock—got involved with some musicians who became famous for both their music and drug use. Walden House, a drug rehabilitation facility in San Francisco is mentioned in *Deathflash*. Gav spent eighteen months rehabbing in that facility. He went through the whole cycle: dabbling with drugs, addiction, rehab, relapse, rehab. The drug chapters in *Deathflash* are all authentic, Gav, my expert, showing me around. I've been to a few AA meeting and many more NA meetings with him (they are not depressing, actually the opposite, inspiring). He is clean and sober now, but still goes to weekly meetings, knowing his susceptibility to the effect of drinking even one beer. Before I knew much about heroin addiction, I figured, like many in law enforcement, that junkies are experiencing what they deserve, should be jailed. But I learned about the "Disease Model" of addiction, and no one, especially a young person, deserves to die for their drug use/disease. I personally support Walden House financially, and donated a number of copies of *Deathflash* for staff and clients.

BES: You've been with Katy Green and Johnny Cato for some time now. Describe how Katy Green developed as a protagonist and how she's changed with you through the years. How about Johnny?

GON: In the past, I've loved reading mystery/thriller books like Michael Connelly's Harry Bosch series or John Sanford's Lucas Davenport series. These are rough/tough masculine detectives, not against taking the law into their own hands when called for. So, I decided to try my hand in this genre. But I wanted something different as not many women are written of as lead detectives. I wrote the first one, modeling Katy Green after my daughter, who is smart, thoughtful, feisty, and tough. But Katy, who went to Sacramento State as I did, is also a basketball player and a struggling writer, too. Some of me in her character. As the books progressed so did Katy, spending more time writing, eventually going full time. She pulls away from her writing to help her partner Johnny Cato solve some murders. It's obvious by the last book, *A Stick of Doublemint*, that she is a successful writer, writing/publishing a number of books with maybe familiar titles.

BES: In the last decade, we've seen major progress in the long struggle to bust open the canon and make room for women, racial minorities, LGBTQ people, and many others so long kept outside. Movements like #Metoo and the "woke" activism represented by the Pussyhat Project, on the other hand, have some critics arguing they at best polarize and at worst demonize or even aim to destroy men and all things masculine. Your body of work includes a great many subjects and characters in the great masculine traditions, and also many strong female characters and subtle, ambiguous themes. What's your take on the changes going on now, particularly in relation to your handling of those primal, primordial things called sex and gender in your work overall and perhaps also specifically in regard to Katy Green?

GON: Well, I'm not much of a philosopher, but of course I'm aware of social changes and concerns. People often mention about my work in general that there are no clear-cut heroes and villains. And not much introspection by the main characters. I worked with young people with special needs, and sprinkle my work with characters who can't speak easily for themselves. Kind of how I see life. I remember something author Damon Knight told me: "If you have a message use Western Union; but if you must, tell an accessible, good story, and in the end, sneak in a punch to the gut." I guess the above character, Harry Bosch, best sums up my philosophy about current social concerns about various people outside: "Everybody counts or nobody counts."

BES: Many of your stories feature settings and characters inspired by your own experiences, or even are based on actual people or events. Which ones stand out as having strange or unique real life connections?

GON: In the late '70s or early '80s, I was the VP at a small insulation manufacturing plant in San Jose. We were busy and by necessity were forced to make insulation blowing machines our customers couldn't get. I set up the program at the plant, hiring a manufacturing crew, which included paroled welders trained in San Quentin. George, our foreman of this program was also an ex-con. It went well, until one day I noticed one of our welders missing. "He didn't call in, George. Where is he?" George shrugged, made a sad face, and said, "He got busted, his parole revoked, cops think he's the *Good Samaritan Rapist.*" He wasn't heavy-set. But years later I based Double Jack (from the same-named novella) on this young guy.

BES: The epilogue to *Deathflash* includes follow-ups for the main characters in the book, as well as Katy and Johnny. Do you plan to return to these characters again, or has their story "ended" here?

GON: I hadn't thought too much about it. But I probably assumed the novels *Shadow of the Dark Angel* and *Deathflash* were the end of the

Green Hornet and Cato. But then I was asked to flesh out a scene in *Shadow* that turned into the novella *Double Jack*. Recently, I found the idea of doing something with the idea of "taking retribution" compelling enough to generate a story. The idea of "an eye for an eye" having justifying moral weight or simply a crime under the law? The novella *A Stick of Doublemint* resulted in the fourth book in the series. So, I don't know if this is finally the end. I do know Katy would like to be able to concentrate exclusively on her writing.

BES: You're part of the post-war "Baby Boom" generation, many of whom are now either facing the Great Unknown, i.e. death, or have already taken that trip. As an artist and a writer, what preoccupies you the most at this phase? What essential things have remained, what hasn't, and what's remained but changed?

GON: Well, like most of my living contemporaries I probably have dwelled too much on death and dying. Seems natural. In the past the question "Is this the end or not" has intrigued me enough to examine it in stories. I've speculated on the Catholic idea of purgatory in a short story called, "In the Big Window." I've examined death in a large number of stories. But the "and then" preoccupies me. Not so much that like others, I've become a Born Again Christian. I'm not religious, but I think I've become spiritual. I think whatever my contemporaries' beliefs, especially those already in ill health, I see a lot of depression. Not so much in my case. I pretty much run about the same every day, mostly focusing on the joy of writing. As far as a sustaining philosophy, it's kind of the underlying spiritual essence in the advice of Warren Zevon, during his last appearance on the Letterman Show before he died: "Enjoy every sandwich."

BES: Talk about your legacy of work. What do you still wish for, and what are you leaving us with?

GON: Legacy is a tough question for any writer to state about his own work. We always look subjectively. I like to think I concentrated on the common man's grand struggles. Not as a hero or a villain, just a person doing their best with what they have to work with. I would hope that I'd see more critical emphasis on what I believe is important in a literary sense in the structure of my work, "voice" and "tone." I try to think about both when writing. I think critics have fairly recognized the importance of character and place in every piece of my work. I hope the last two novel-length series I will do will be considered my best, both critics and fans enjoying *The White Plague Chronicles*—it's all there.

(February 6, 2020)

———

B.E. Scully lives in a crooked red house that lacks a foundation in the misty woods of Oregon with a variety of human and animal companions. Scully is the author of numerous novels, short stories, poems, and articles. Published work, interviews, and odd scribblings can be found at www.bescully.com.

ALSO FROM DARK MOON BOOKS:

EXPLORING DARK SHORT FICTION #2: A PRIMER TO KAARON WARREN

Australian author Kaaron Warren is widely recognized as one of the leading writers today of speculative and dark short fiction. She's published four novels, multiple novellas, and well over one hundred heart-rending tales of horror, science fiction, and beautiful fantasy, and is the first author ever to simultaneously win all three of Australia's top speculative fiction writing awards (Ditmar, Shadows, and Aurealis awards for *The Grief Hole*).

Dark Moon Books and editor Eric J. Guignard bring you this introduction to her work, the second in a series of primers exploring modern masters of literary dark short fiction. Herein is a chance to discover—or learn more of—the distinct voice of Kaaron Warren, as beautifully illustrated by artist Michelle Prebich.

Included within these pages are:
- Six short stories, one written exclusively for this book
- Author interview
- Complete bibliography
- Academic commentary by Michael Arnzen, PhD (former humanities chair and professor of the year, Seton Hill University)
- . . . and more!

Enter this doorway to the vast and fantastic: Get to know Kaaron Warren.

Order your copy at www.darkmoonbooks.com or www.amazon.com
ISBN-13: 978-0-9989383-0-1

ABOUT THE AUTHOR

Gene O'Neill has seen over 175 of his stories and novellas published, several also reprinted in France, Spain, and Russia. Some of these stories have been collected in *Ghost Spirits, Computers & World Machines; The Grand Struggle; In Dark Corners; Dance of the Blue Lady; The Hitchhiking Effect;* and *Lethal Birds*. In addition, he's published six novels. Gene has been a Bram Stoker Award® finalist twelve times. In 2010 *Taste of Tenderloin* won the

Photograph by Jason V Brock

haunted house for collection, and in 2012 *The Blue Heron* won for Long Fiction. Upcoming in 2017 are the four trade paperback versions of the *Cal Wild Chronicles* from Written Backwards Press, a number of short stories, and a novelette. A long novel, *The White Plague Chronicles*, is a work in progress, parts to an interested publisher.

Gene lives in the Napa Valley with his wife, Kay. He has two grown children, Gavin, who lives in Oakland, and Kaydee who lives in Carlsbad and rides herd on his two grandchildren, Fiona and TJ.

When he isn't writing or visiting grandchildren, Gene likes to read good fiction or watch sports—all of them, especially boxing.